T0128437

Janine B. Hegle

Dressed in Fine Linen

The Daze of Adulting

Illustrations by Mireille Mann

WESTBOW
PRESS®
A DIVISION OF THOMAS NELSON
& ZONDERVAN

THE HOLY BIBLE, NEW INTERNATIONAL VERSION®, NIV® Copyright © 1973, 1978, 1984, 2011 by Biblica, Inc.® Used by permission. All rights reserved worldwide.

WestBow Press books may be ordered through booksellers or by contacting:

WestBow Press
A Division of Thomas Nelson & Zondervan
1663 Liberty Drive
Bloomington, IN 47403
www.westbowpress.com
1 (866) 928-1240

ISBN: 978-1-9736-5701-9 (sc)
ISBN: 978-1-9736-5700-2 (hc)
ISBN: 978-1-9736-5702-6 (e)

Library of Congress Control Number: 2019903136

Print information available on the last page.

WestBow Press rev. date: 04/03/2019

about the book

"What are you going to do when you graduate?" was the question Erica dreaded answering. That is, until she took Margie up on her passing invitation to move across the States to live in Dallas. Yes, she'll have something exciting to tell people. But, with any situation that arises out of impulse more than plan, trouble soon ensues as she begins to design a life for herself.

What's going on behind--the-scenes as Erica's morals get defined, her emotions pique, and relationships develop? Where are the challenges coming from and who or what is shaping her life? With a much yearned-for independence, Erica still fights against all the newness, at times, seeking the familiar. Through many highs and lows, Erica Webb is learning what it's like to live with herself and to contend for her faith.

Enter the journey of life after graduation.

chapter one

After twenty years of preparation, Erica knew this was not just some final psych exam to check whether or not the material had been mastered. It was not merely a business practicum that was being assessed. It was the real deal. Life. Adult life. *Adulting.*

The college years could be summed up by a scale—a few pounds up, a few pounds down—and no, Erica never did get those designer jeans from her now-ex that had been promised to her when she reached 120 pounds again. But graduation day was now in the past, and with a big move, her life was going to really happen. Packing up had been easy enough. The sadness of goodbyes had been mixed with the excitement of a new adventure. Even Erica couldn't believe she was really going to do something so cool as drive across the country and then job hunt—going but not knowing what would happen.

Erica got into her hatchback to drive halfway across the United States. Her small New Jersey community nestled among trees would soon be several hours away, with no return date in mind.

With a BA, a new Nissan, readiness for life, and her I-get-to-make-my-own-decisions-now resolve, Erica found herself coasting into yet another gas station, this time in Tennessee. She was hit by yet another accent. It was a truly defining moment. She had left the Northeast, and now she knew it. New Jersey suddenly seemed farther away than just a few hours. It was "Goodbye, Yankees. Hello, rednecks."

Destination Dallas accomplished, but not without a few mishaps. Nailing the whole downshifting thing was still a challenge, especially going from highway to gas station. Tall buildings, open air, and an abundance of sunshine filled her eyes. Everything looked so new, so modern, so fresh, until she drove up to her apartment complex. The scenery around it was great; her own apartments were the eyesore. Erica parked her car right next to a blue one. She had found her parking spot with ease. Now to find Margie and use the bathroom.

"Erica, up here!" shouted Margie.

"What a relief to see you. I need to pee." Then we can unload this stuff and get some supper. I'm starving."

"I have a doctor's appointment at seven o'clock, but I still have a few minutes to help unload. Trade you the car key for the apartment door so I can start unloading your car while you unload that bladder."

By 7:10, Erica found herself surrounded by boxes, her dresser drawers, two laundry baskets of clothes, cosmetics, hanging clothes, and no one to talk to. She quickly texted her parents of her safe arrival. She had planned on eating out, but with no one in town that she knew besides Margie, she filled up on water and some Triscuits with peanut butter. The closet was full, so she left her hanging clothes on the couch. She found her gray silk sheets, made the bed, and then took a shower to get rid of the stickies and stinkies of travel and unpacking.

Erica's first days of job hunting had been hectic. Today, she had checked out a drug rehab counseling center that immediately intimidated her, then several data entry positions in pursuit of a career in business. Wearing high heels had not been the wisest choice, and now her feet were aching from all the walking and standing around, but she had to put that behind her. She was looking forward to her evening. She opened the door to her new apartment. Her roommate had never job hunted, since she'd landed a position while still in college with an architectural firm just down the road.

"Hey, Margie," Erica said, "you look so relaxed. How long have you been home?"

Margie was comfortably enmeshed in both the couch and her book, but she mustered up the effort to respond. "Since 4:30. Find any work?"

"Not officially, but I should have a job in no time. I found plenty of great leads today. In the morning, I interviewed at a finance company in downtown Dallas." Erica took a quick breath and continued, "And this afternoon, I had a great interview at a new company just around the corner—at the LBJ and Central intersection. Oh, and I stopped in at a temp place next to where I ate lunch. I did the keyboarding test thing there. I guess traipsing all over town will be my life until I get a full-time job, but it's so much fun visiting all these places, seeing all the new faces, and seeing all the opportunities available out here. I may just miss days like today."

It had been a taxing day, but Erica still had an energy that naturally exuded from her.

"So what was your day like?"

Margie yawned, lifting a hand toward the kitchen. "There's defrosted chicken in the fridge. Make what you want. I'm not hungry."

Erica noticed that Margie hadn't answered her question. "Thanks, but I'll be out with Mitch tonight. He said he'd show me around Dallas. Thanks again for introducing me to him. He seems like such a sweet guy." Erica glanced at her watch. "I had better get in the shower. Uh, he should be here soon. Oh, by the way, do you have any plans for tonight?"

"Just my book," replied Margie.

Erica closed the bedroom door and proceeded to get ready for her date. She wondered if Margie was okay with her being out so late every night, but Erica had so much she wanted to know about the city. She didn't want to miss out on anything.

Gross. Erica noticed roaches frolicking near her makeup and toothbrush. Disgusted, she flicked several of them off the bathroom counter. Then she rinsed off her toothbrush with piping hot water and got busy removing her makeup residue before brushing her teeth.

The cool shower water cascading down her shoulders was almost refreshing, but she was perspiring again before she could even grab a towel to dry off. The Dallas nights didn't seem to cool off at all. If May was this bad, what would July and August be like?

Erica was almost ready when she heard Mitch and Margie talking. Curiosity was killing her, so she opened the bedroom door to get a peek while buckling on her purple high-heeled sandals.

"Hey there, Mitch. I see you wasted no time."

"Evening, Margie." Like a gentleman, Mitch remained at the door, but after a long silence, he asked, "May I come in?"

"Yup."

"Guess you heard I have a date with Erica."

"Yup."

"So you're reading another Dan Brown novel. Popular book. What do you think about it?"

"Not done yet."

"You really trek through the books. I don't seem to read much fiction these days. Seminary keeps me pretty busy."

Erica entered from the adjacent room. "I'm so sorry to keep you waiting. I'm glad Margie was here to keep you company. So what adventure do you have planned for us tonight?"

"What would you say if I told you we're going to a renovated schoolhouse?"

"*Ummm*, sounds enchanting?" Erica was confused. "When you said you'd show me around town, I guess I had something else in mind."

"It's a really cool restaurant. All the waiters and waitresses dress like famous people. The menu is quite creative, and so are the eating areas. You'll see. Costs a mint, but you'll never forget where you went on your first expensive date with me—guaranteed! Well, we should be going. Bye, Margie."

Margie gave a nod as Erica and Mitch left.

chapter two

Mitch saw the blinking light, so he pushed the button. "Mitch, I need to talk to you. Please, please call me when you get home."

This was the second message Erica had left on Mitch's machine today. He didn't really like it when girls came on too strong. Erica was coming across as a bit too aggressive for Mitch, but he decided to go ahead and call her back, realizing it might be important.

"Hello?" she said.

"Hi. It's Mitch. You said you needed to talk. What's up?"

"Oh, Mitch, my head is just spinning, and my body is shaking. I'm so excited. I can't believe it, but I got offered jobs at both companies. Two offers my first week. And my dad thought it'd never happen. Granted, we're not talking big bucks, but it's my first real job. *Yesss!*"

"That's exciting news. I'm happy for you. What kind of package are they offering you?" Mitch immediately realized he came across more as a businessman looking to the bottom line than a seminary student, so he quickly added, "'Praise the Lord."

"Both are just entry-level positions. I didn't have much to bargain with since my job experience was limited to lifeguard and waitress at camp, department store salesperson, and the few months at Casio." After a quick breath, she continued, "The job close by is offering twelve dollars an hour. It's a small company, kind of a mom-and-pop deal. The other job, downtown, pays $9.40 an hour and is with a big company that employs hundreds in that office alone. The agency will get their commission after I've worked for three months. Perhaps then I can negotiate for more pay. So which one do you think I should take?"

"I don't—"

She cut him off. "I keep thinking about working downtown. It seems so exciting. The idea of ever working in New York City seemed overwhelming to me, but I think I can handle Dallas. I'm young and single, so why not go for the big company with potential to meet lots of people?"

"Sounds like you made your decision."

"But then I think about the other company. The people were so personable, so sweet, and I could get in on a ground floor and work my way up. The office was gorgeous too—beautiful woodwork throughout the building. It might end up being like an extended family for me."

"Guess you need to sleep on it. Hey, are we still on for breakfast tomorrow?" Mitch interjected.

"You bet. I better try and get some sleep. Hey, thanks for listening. See you at 8:30."

Mitch felt satisfied with the call. He fell asleep after praying about Erica's big decision, and he considered the idea of dating her more seriously. Maybe she wasn't the needy female he had feared. She sure had a presence he couldn't resist. Even over the phone, he could picture the way her eyes lit up her face. Her blonde, shoulder-length hair and curvaceous figure had caught his attention initially, but it was her enthusiasm and carefree nature that made him want to pursue a relationship with her.

Maybe he was jumping the gun, but everyone's heard of love at first sight, right? And it wouldn't be so popular if it wasn't so common. Yes, Erica was a girl worth pursuing. That he was sure of.

chapter three

It was June 19 and Erica's fourth week on the job downtown. Almost everyone on the team showed up to do their assigned task. Delia, the receptionist, apparently took the whole day off for a doctor's appointment. Erica did a double-take when she saw Josie come to work with curlers still in her hair, but at least she came. Josie was always missing from work on Mondays; rumor was she needed Mondays to get over her customary weekend hangover. Peering around the room, Erica noticed Jolene wearing a stunning black leather vest and her usual tight jeans. Then there were Erica's three bosses: Roger seemed preoccupied and just not his usual self. Judith's makeup job was over-the-top (again), and Rusty did his usual cordial nodding to whatever was said or to whoever passed by; nothing too exciting was happening at work.

Erica was going for her sixth cup of coffee and had been to the bathroom twice, and the clock hadn't even registered the 10 a.m. break yet. Business was always slow to dead until the checks came in. But after they arrived, it turned into hyper-hustle time: process the checks, get them deposited, write up the reports, make another much-needed trip to the bathroom, breathe a sigh of relief, fill the coffee cup a few more times, and endure till quitting time. That was the routine.

By quitting time, everyone working downtown was anxious to get on the bus and get home, so finding something to do after work (besides beelining it home) was usually a good idea. The choice was to stand and wait for a bus as the sun beat down on the crowd on the sidewalk, or to sit and relax in the comfort of an air-conditioned office for another forty minutes. Erica's budget was tight, so she usually just stayed on at the office instead of checking out the local shops.

Today Erica was e-mailing family and friends back East while changing her nail polish and listening to her iPod.

Jolene stopped at Erica's desk as she was hitting the Send button. "Care to join me for a drink?" she asked.

The empty look in Jolene's eyes made Erica feel uncomfortable. It dawned on her that there was another alternative end-of-the-day activity—the local bar. She had said "me" and not "us." This made Erica even more uncomfortable.

"Oh, thanks," Erica began, hesitating, "but I'll have to be going soon."

Usually, Erica declined such offers out of principle, but today she realized her reply was rooted in fear more than principle. She hadn't really thought of socializing with Jolene before then, but the panic grew as she realized she'd be clueless to even know what type of drink to order. She'd heard of rum and Coke, but she didn't know if she'd like it. Her friend once suggested she order a Tom Collins, but that was when she was underage. Did it even have alcohol in it? She felt unprepared for her first happy hour. Yet as Jolene walked away, Erica recalled Jolene's strained voice and the look in her eyes. This wouldn't be a very happy hour for Jolene. Jolene probably needed the company, but all Erica could think about was preserving her own ego and getting home. She continued to double-guess her decision. Could she have been a friend to Jolene?

The bus ride home seemed to take forever. Erica figured she had better leave work a half-hour earlier than usual since she had told Jolene she had to get going. Central Avenue was pure standstill, as predicted. Erica didn't like all the traffic of a big city, nor the long lines everywhere— at the banks, the DMV, and every check-out counter. City life had its drawbacks. If it wasn't the issue of long lines, it was the stress of finding a parking spot, then having to pay for it. It was difficult to find an affordable place to get her hair cut, and she didn't know where to start to find a dentist or a doctor if she needed one, nor did she know what she should consider in choosing one.

Erica finally noticed her boss, Roger. He had a seat on the same bus, just two people away. He looked relaxed, having taken off his tie and suit coat, and he was doing his best to cool off. Roger was always working—still looking at his computer screen as he traveled. He didn't notice her, but he was definitely worth noticing—all six feet of him. After the second stop, Erica was able to find a seat. The lady she sat next to was obviously a smoker and seemed to love perfume—cheap perfume. Erica's eyes soon felt scratchy and irritated. It was not working for her.

Erica continued stewing about the fact that she knew Margie was already home, relaxed and stress-free. Feeling irritated and fighting a growing bitterness, Erica pictured Margie's obituary: "Margie Brown, brunette Caucasian, resident of Dallas, Texas, was found dead in her living room; her book was open to page 287, but all who knew her said she died doing what she loved best." Yeah, that's what it would say. And what was her most recent book? That's right; she was reading another murder mystery.

Erica never read for pleasure. Her mom always apologized for not reading to her more as a child, but she didn't care. TV had pictures, books didn't. Plus, she always got tired and headachy after only five minutes of reading, and her mind always wandered away from the black and white on the pages. She could turn page after page before she'd realize she had no clue what was on them. However, during her last semester of college, she discovered she had astigmatism and found glasses did help with the tiredness and headaches. Margie's ability to relax with a book was challenging Erica's thoughts about giving books another try.

It was nearing six o'clock. Erica got off the bus. The three-minute walk home was most difficult, as her head was pounding, and her hot, reddened face seemed ready to explode. She arrived home all sweaty and sticky, walked right through the empty living room, grabbed a box of tissues, and fell face down on her bed. A dam of tears finally broke free from her façade of strength. Her tired, achy body and weary mind gave way to self-pity. She questioned whether she'd made the right decision about her job choice—she was so bored at work. She'd had doubts about the wisdom of moving to Dallas. Her dad had said it'd be hard to find a job with so many unemployed. Ha. She had found one her first week. But was it the right one? Then there was her no-win situation with Jolene today. Erica wondered why she'd ever chosen a lower-paying job farther away, with a bunch of people she had nothing in common with.

Her stinky, smoke-stenched body was getting to her as much as her stinky life. The apartment was always sweltering hot, but she didn't have enough money to pay for the A/C, so she had to endure the heat and humidity. Margie apparently was used to the Dallas heat and appreciated saving every possible cent for a new car. Erica would just have to live with the heat, the roaches, her long bus rides home, and the ramifications of her grown-up-world decisions.

She was coming to realize that no one around her really knew her, no one in her daily life cared about her, and no one had as much as touched her since she had moved away from her family. Of course, there was Roger from work and his flattery, but that was just a temporary fix to cheer her up. Alone in a world of strangers, she yearned for a reminder that she was still a human being. She felt—she felt—disconnected. She felt empty. And then, for a moment, she felt absolutely nothing, and it sort of scared her.

She knew she needed to stop this wallowing, so she showered. Feeling hungry, she went to the kitchen, melted some Swiss cheese on a hotdog in the microwave, and scrounged around the cupboard for some real food. Finding nothing of interest, she ate another hotdog with melted Swiss while flipping channels. Nothing on but *Seinfeld* reruns. Hopefully, *Seinfeld* would do the trick.

That same evening, Margie was out late. It was 10:30 p.m. when Erica gave up on trying to sleep. Her stomach was hurting, and her thoughts were centered on herself. Today, even Mitch seemed like an annoyance. At first, she liked all his calls, but they were revealing a man desperately looking for a wife. It was like a salesman trying to close a deal before really making the sale. He lacked in the romance department—no gifts, no flowers, no notes— yet she could tell that he wanted a wife in the worst way. Seems the pressure is really on those seminary guys to get married. Most churches won't chance hiring a handsome single guy to be a pastor. Seems it's one of those jobs where the wife factor is a biggie.

Erica lay on her bed thinking and eventually got around to relaxing. Her mind was again on Mitch. Handsome Mitch. Interesting Mitch. Mitch with the dreamy eyes— eyes she could get lost in. And Mitch, Mr. Wonderful-to-Talk-to-Mitch. So why had she just been complaining? What didn't he have? Oh yeah, a wife.

It was 10:50 p.m. when Margie finally arrived home.

"Hey, where you been?" Erica asked. "I was getting worried about you. You're never out this late."

Margie's simple reply was, "The police station."

"Oh?" Erica was as equally curious as she was concerned, so she tried to get a good look at Margie, but her roommate quickly disappeared into the bathroom without another word.

Something seemed very wrong, but Erica didn't think she should push it. Margie was a mystery to her. If fact, she was downright mysterious. Erica had never known anyone to speak so few words. The why haunted Erica.

chapter four

The bus wasn't very full yet, but by Royal Lane, there would barely be standing room. Roger stood up and moved over to a seat to be with someone he knew. "May I sit here, Miss Webb?" he asked.

"Why, of course, my pleasure," she replied; she hadn't been able to talk with Roger lately during her lunch break, so this would be a doubly nice way to pass the time. This was the first chance they had to sit together going to work, allowing them to actually converse for half an hour (instead of the quick five minutes between Royal Lane and her stop, when seats were again available on the return trip).

"What is it that you are studying?" Roger asked.

"Oh, I was just reviewing prayer requests for a friend I pray for."

"I better not disturb you, then."

"I'll just be a minute."

Erica tried to pray, but it felt like an artificial display of spirituality with Roger's presence so immanent. She cut her prayer time short and decided to chat with Roger.

"So, how's the big deal coming along? You've seemed

so distracted these past two weeks. I've missed our usual strategizing chats."

"Well, you probably need to pray for *me*. I don't think we're going to get the contract. We'll know by tomorrow, since their deadline is June 30." Roger sighed, and then added, "I put so many hours into this proposal; I'll be really ticked if those execs don't sign. We're offering them a really good deal already, and they keep demanding revisions. I think they're just playing with us."

"Sorry to hear that. No fun feeling like all your effort might be wasted." Erica told Roger she'd pray for him.

The awkward silence was getting to Erica. She wanted to encourage Roger, but how?

"I was noticing your wedding ring," she said. "It's one of the nicest guys' rings I've ever seen. I like all the diamonds."

"I don't like it," he said.

She was bewildered. She wondered if he thought it wasn't manly enough. "And why not, may I ask?"

"You really want to know? It's because it keeps me from dating women like you."

"Oh."

Erica gulped and stared downward, trying to control her breathing, pretending to herself that she hadn't just heard what she knew she had. It was only 7:30 a.m., and her very handsome boss was hitting on her. Goodness, she was still half-asleep, and this was not what she had planned for on her ride to work. Sure, she usually looked forward to his encouraging comments, his flattery, but this was downright inappropriate. What was he thinking?

He's got a wife and kids. Doesn't that mean anything to him? At twenty-eight, he's too young for a midlife crisis. It just didn't make sense.

The rest of Erica's day was spent in a daze of unbelief as she relived the interaction over and over in her mind. At 2:30, it was time to take all the newly updated case files to the bosses.

"Rusty, here are today's checks, all ready for deposit." Erica plopped the files on the edge of Rusty's desk. "I'll get the rest of the paperwork to you before your meeting. I just have to draft a letter of explanation for the fifth account."

"Great," Rusty said. "Keep up the good work. I appreciate all you do here."

Rusty was such a gentle, sweet man. Sure, his hair was thinning and his pants were starting to be worn old-man style, but he had a sweet grandpa way about him that would put a smile on anyone's face. Erica liked the simplicity of working for a sixty-four-year-old man. Rusty kept pictures of his wife, his only son, and his five grandchildren and their mates on his desk. He also kept everyone up-to-date on his soon-to-arrive great-grandson. It'd be his first. Rusty would retire soon, and Erica wondered if she'd be offered his job.

Erica walked over to Judith's desk and gave her some checks, as well. Erica couldn't understand why Judith insisted on wearing her hair in a 1960s-style beehive; it looked so out of date. She was sweet but definitely out of touch when it came to fashion. On to Roger's desk. Erica both dreaded and desired going to Roger's desk since his early morning announcement.

"I have your checks ready." She kept the conversation formal.

"You really do look lovely today," he said. "Another new outfit? My, my."

"Yeah, I guess." She wanted to ignore him, so she downplayed the issue. Sure, it felt good to have someone notice these little things, but now it seemed so wrong.

"I have a riddle for you. What's better than a rose …" His voice trailed off into a whisper she almost couldn't hear.

Erica didn't guess the answer to the riddle. "I give up? What's the answer?"

She didn't even catch on to the answer at first, but when she did, her face flushed red. Her naivety was showing. Disgusted, Erica blurted out, "You have a lot of nerve, telling me such a crude joke."

"You love it, and you know it." Roger chuckled.

Erica wondered if that were true. "I do not. I think you have me all wrong."

"Do I? You prance around here in your alluring clothing, and you're quite talented with those flirty eyes of yours. What's a man to think? Oh, you may not say it out loud, but you want me."

"Give me a break. And I dress stylish, not alluring. Look at what I'm wearing—a pale green skirt and a matching top with an innocent country-girl look. Sheesh, the skirt goes all the way down to my ankles."

"Ah, but the slit goes up your left thigh, and the neckline is open, so when you hand me those papers—" He had a gleam in his eyes.

"Only a perv like you would think like that." Erica couldn't believe she'd just said that to one of her bosses.

Roger continued, "Okay, how about that delicate white sundress of yours—a bit skimpy, eh? Or the tight black skirt with the sequins? Or the red top that's rather sheer? Just yesterday, you wore a brown suit, and it had a slit up the back that was very fine, if I say so myself. And then there's the V-neck …"

Erica began to feel dizzy, and Roger's words were fading into a distant haze. This guy was recalling all the clothing she'd worn over the past two weeks. There was an ache in her gut, a sinking feeling. Her forehead started to pound. She loved all her new clothes; to her, they were sharp, cute, funky, stylish.

"… short striped skirt and those sexy four-inch purple strapped heels that let me know you're coming, and—"

Erica finally retorted, "Go find yourself another hobby."

"Is that an invitation?"

"Argggh!"

She left him, trying not to show her fury. She certainly didn't want to be answering any questions from her co-workers, but if she could have, she would have stomped off, slammed the door, flung her chair up high, and flipped another one over. Yep, that's how she imagined her rage in action.

Margie wasn't in the apartment when Erica got home. It was time for Erica to *enjoy* being alone in the apartment, and it carried an enticement of sorts. She felt like a kid in a toyshop. She was suddenly overwhelmed by a sense of freedom she hadn't expected. She could talk out loud or sing or scream; she could dance in the kitchen or sit and watch TV with just a towel on. She mentally continued listing her options. She just wanted Roger out of her head.

She began her evening by turning up the volume on her stereo, plucking her eyebrows, and dreaming of life with Mitch. Dream over, Erica put on her white bikini and headed out to the pool for a swim.

Elaine was already out there, sipping her Friday evening drink of choice. She was really easy to talk to and always hospitable. Erica truly enjoyed Elaine's company, even if they did come from two different worlds. Elaine seemed to entertain gentlemen on an hourly basis, but it was that endearing side to her that kept Erica from just writing her off as a friend. Elaine was a kind-hearted person who lived life the only way she'd knew how. Erica's thoughts went back to the time and attention Elaine put forth just the previous weekend, when she spent four hours putting false nails on Erica's hands just before they did some bargain-hunting.

"Relaxing with your tequila, I see?"

"Yeah. Want one? Just get a glass."

"I was just planning on a swim. Hey, did you see Margie tonight? She wasn't home when I got home."

"No, but maybe Elmer did." Elaine yelled across the pool, "Hey, Elmer, you see Margie this evening?"

"Who's Margie?"

"Lives in 4B. You know, noisy car …"

"Blue car girl?" Elmer started to walk toward the girls.

"Yeah, that's her."

Erica wondered how people would describe her when she wasn't around. Would it be "the girl who goes to church every Sunday" or "the one who always comes home at seven o'clock" or "the girl who's put on a few pounds lately"?

"We haven't officially met. I'm Elmer. Elmer Stud. And your name?"

Chuckling, she responded, "Um—my name is Erica. Nice to meet you. So, what do you do?"

"I stock shelves at Winn Dixie. They like us big Alabama boys."

"You home early today, Elmer? Don't you usually work evenings?" interjected Elaine.

"Today I didn't go in. I was feeling sick."

Elmer wasted no time changing out of his clothes and joining Erica in the pool. After their swim, Erica ended up helping Elmer and Elaine finish off the new pitcher of Tequila Sunrise.

Erica found this to be the perfect end to her long day. She breathed in the essence of the big southern boy and found herself gravitating to the gentle kindness of Elaine. The radio was playing "As Time Goes By" by Louis Armstrong. Louis's voice soothed her troubled mind, and the breeze and the gentle warmth from the drink engraved this Texas summer night deep in Erica's heart. She sauntered back to her apartment, humming the words still playing in her mind, "a kiss is just a kiss."

chapter five

Erica and Elmer were fast becoming friends. Elmer was just out of high school and several years younger than Erica, but they had fun together. Mitch was the official man in Erica's life, but it was so much easier to get to know Elmer since he lived in the same complex. Elmer would get home much later than Erica, but they usually swam together in the pool late in the evening. Today, however, they were relaxing together, working on their Texas tan. Elmer's curly blond hair shimmered as the rays shone down on his already dark, oiled skin.

It hadn't been anything formal; Erica had just finished preparing lots of food and was willing to share. She was trying out some new recipes, and Elmer wasn't doing anything, so he joined her for supper. Elmer had never eaten rice pilaf before, and he made fun of the name. He had never eaten veal before, either. After playing Trump: The Game for a while, they went back into the kitchen for some pumpkin cheesecake.

Leaning against the counter, Elmer said, "I feel something hot, something warm. What's going on?

Something's toasting my buns." He was so confused, but it all sounded so cute in his Alabama twang. "It's just the dishwasher in its drying cycle. Don't you have one?"

Although Elmer was lots of fun to be around, Erica knew from nearly daily encounters that he wasn't her intellectual equal. It was at that moment something clicked. Erica really did like Mitch; the problem was they never did anything fun together. Erica wanted a guy to go on walks with her around the lake, or ride on the paddleboats with her, or shoot pool with her, or play board games with her, or just swim with her. Mitch and Erica needed a playdate.

Elmer finally left around eleven o'clock, and Erica couldn't control herself. She dialed Mitch's cell phone. No answer. Should she dial again? Was he sleeping? Should she chance waking his roommates by calling his other number?

She decided to go to bed, but her busy thoughts and plans prevented a sound sleep.

chapter six

"Just let yourself in, Mitch. Dinner's almost ready."
Erica was busy draining the pasta. "Look through the
DVDs and see if there's something you want to watch."
"Well, hello to you, too." Mitch's sarcastic comment
was muffled. Was wanting her to actually greet him
expecting too much?
"Sorry, I can't hear you. You can join me in the kitchen
if you want."
Erica started up the beaters so the whipped cream
would be all ready for dessert.
Mitch realized she was busy, so he decided to
leaf through some magazines. He could tell from the
placement of the candles that Erica wanted to make the
evening special for them both, and he wanted the same.
He didn't want it to be just a veg-and-watch-a-movie
night. After all, it would be their first time together at
the apartment without Margie around. She was off to a
business convention in Mesquite that would last until the
early morning hours.
Mitch was flipping through a back issue of Margie's
Architectural Digest when something caught his attention.
It was definitely Erica's handwriting on some very

familiar-looking stationery. Mitch liked the way Erica would write notes and letters in this technologically driven age of e-mails and instant messaging. At first, he just glanced at it, then he started to read the letter.

May 1ˢᵗ

Dear Margie,

I am so excited about coming to live with you. Your invitation was just what I needed so I could have something interesting to tell people upon graduating. EVERYBODY asks!

It's been a long time since we've hung out. Well, we'll just have to get reacquainted. I know we'll have a blast together.

I should be arriving on May 7.

I'm a nervous wreck. I bought a car, but it has standard transmission, and I still have to figure out how to drive it. The downshifting seems to be the tough part. A friend at college let me drive around in his car. The first day, he couldn't figure out why I was having so much trouble. Well, after lots of starts and stops, he realized I still had the emergency brake on. Ditz, I know. But I was consoled that it took him so long to figure it out.

So, see you in a few days,
Erica

Mitch met Margie at a Christmas party during his first year of seminary. So it was immediately clear to him from the letter that Erica had no clue about the real Margie. Margie wouldn't be looking for a close, best-friend type of relationship, but it appeared that Erica was thinking that would happen.

"Dinner is ready. Come help me take it into the living room."

"Be right there." Mitch tucked the letter back into the magazine and placed it back on the coffee table.

Erica was organized, and in just seconds, they were ready to eat. Mitch nervously said a prayer. They were holding hands for the first time, and when it came time to release their hands, he knew they had entered uncharted territory. Dinner conversation centered on their family backgrounds, until Erica brought up the topic of doing fun things together.

"I just don't have much money, Erica." Mitch knew she might be high-maintenance, but he'd tried to ignore that.

"Walks around the lake don't cost much. Rollerblading is free after the initial purchase. We can just have cheap thrills."

The comment lessened the tension that had begun to rise, but Mitch knew it was time to shift the conversation to something else.

He asked, "So what kind of expectations did you have for a relationship—with Margie?"

He could see he caught Erica off-guard—that she'd be thinking he'd want to continue to talk about *them*. However, she seemed to adjust her thoughts to the new topic.

"Well, I met Margie through her brother, Stephen. He was a senior who dated my college roommate, Koren. And since he had a car, he'd load it up with friends whenever he went home, and then we'd enjoy home-cooked meals his mom would make. It was a real treat. I think I went along at least once a month. That's when I met Margie. Expectations, eh? I guess I shouldn't have had any since I didn't know her that well."

"But you did have some, I bet. So what's it like between you two? Seems like there's tension."

"Not really tension—just nothing. For example, back in June, she came home late one night. When I asked where she'd been, she answered, 'The police station.' I didn't feel I could pry, but I've wondered what was up. She's seemed ... well, I can't really describe it."

The conversation continued for a few minutes, documenting their history together, but then it went on to other things, ending with a promise of a phone call in the morning.

chapter seven

For the next month, Roger continued to harass Erica at work. She wrestled over the decision to quit before the three-month mark of August 29; she knew she had to do something about the situation. She couldn't continue to live under the pressure of Roger's enticements. Oh, there had been days that could have been viewed as normal, just like this particular Thursday turned out. Initially, she thought she'd quit her job after a rough couple of days of dealing with her temptations and struggles with Roger. But as it turned out, Roger made a fun bet with Erica and Jolene the day before, and the loser had to pay for lunch. Roger lost (they all knew he would), and he took the two out for an extended lunch at the Spaghetti Warehouse. It was a wonderful break from work, delightful to have a free meal, and nothing crossed the line. It made Erica second-guess her plan to quit. By the time they got back to work, it was time to go home. Although Erica walked over to the office of Carl Ramsey, the vice president, she decided to postpone that visit after all. She rationalized that if life could go on like it did today, she would be able to stay there. She got her things and headed home.

Elmer surprised Erica when she got home. Earlier that day, he had switched shifts with Margo, a co-worker who needed to attend a wake for her uncle. An hour later, Erica and Elmer left to grab a quick bite. Erica insisted they go Dutch, since Elmer wasn't a Christian, and it wasn't a date. However, it still felt like one, and Erica had to admit that much to herself. As usual, they did have a bunch of fun. Their evening ended with two rounds of bowling and a few games of pool. Erica did much better playing pool than bowling, but Elmer beat her in both.

It was after midnight before they got back. After they parted ways, Elmer remembered he still had Erica's keys in his pocket. He got her attention just as she reached the top stair to her apartment. He held her keys high and jingled them in the air. She hit her temple with the palm of her hand and rapidly descended the steps. Elmer handed her the keys, accompanied by a big, huge bear hug, right out in the open.

Erica thought it was sweet but was wondering who might be watching; that is, until he planted a delicious and sensuous kiss on her lips and kept it there. To her surprise, she melted in his big ol' Southern arms. She thought she had just been transported to a movie screen, and to be honest, she was ready to make the moment last and keep her audience enthralled. Her legs turned to jelly, and it was only Elmer's arms that kept her standing. Any sense of logic was gone. Any thoughts of the ramifications of her actions were gone. Any thoughts of ... Oh, no. Mitch. What was she thinking?

She chose to put those thoughts on hold and stay in the dreamlike moment.

chapter eight

Picking up the phone, she heard, "Erica, it's David, Elmer's roommate. How are you?"

"Doing okay. Hey, you've never called before. What's up?"

"I'm going to meet Elmer at a dance club off Central Avenue. After all, we have to have some fun over this Labor Day weekend, right? He wants me to convince you to come along. Are you interested? I'll leave here at 7:30, and you can drive with me."

Erica knew she just wanted Elmer as a friend, and she didn't want to lead him on. Although she had replayed the kiss from the previous week over and over and over again, she blocked out any feelings of fault. She was a victim as far as she was concerned, and it wouldn't happen again.

"David, I don't know the first thing about dancing. I don't think so."

"Elmer will be really disappointed. Anyway, it's usually so crowded, no one really dances. You have anything better to do?"

No, in fact, she didn't have *anything* to do. Mitch had gone to his cousin's wedding, and she didn't even have a book to read. She could use this opportunity to set Elmer straight and let him know that all he should expect from her was a friendship. It seemed like a golden opportunity.

"I guess I don't have anything on my calendar … yet."

"So, come."

"What should I wear?"

"Jeans—just go casual."

"Okay, see you at 7:30."

She placed the phone down, wondering what she'd gotten herself in to, but she knew one thing: it'd be fun, at least until she had her talk with Elmer.

She was in the middle of putting on her mascara when the phone rang again.

She shuffled over to the answering machine in the adjacent room, grabbing the phone like she was fumbling over a football. "Hello. Hello? Anyone there?"

"I'm here."

While still attempting to catch her balance, she eked out, "Mitch, don't hang up."

"Oh, I've missed you so much." Mitch hadn't hung up, and his words were sweet, like a Godiva chocolate-covered strawberry.

"How are you? How was the wedding? I've missed you, too." Erica was finally sitting down.

"I'm good. The wedding was sweet. My cousin really loves this guy; that was plain to see. I just kept wishing you were there to share the day with me."

"Trust me, I would have if I could have."

"I don't want to run up the bill, so I'll say good-bye. Remember, my flight arrives at 1:40 p.m. on Sunday. Plan for a late lunch, okay?"

"You bet. I can't wait. Bye."

"Bye, sweetness."

Erica had wanted to go along with Mitch, but since the wedding was on a Thursday, she had to decline. She reoriented her thinking back to getting ready to go out. She had her jeans picked out, but she was struggling over which shirt to wear. She didn't want to send any wrong messages. The peach shirt was the winner—soft and innocent.

"The door! He's here early."

When Erica opened the door, she saw two men in uniform and assumed they were selling tickets to a fundraiser.

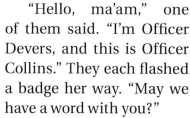

"Hello, ma'am," one of them said. "I'm Officer Devers, and this is Officer Collins." They each flashed a badge her way. "May we have a word with you?"

"Excuse me, officer. I was expecting my friend David and not a visit from the police. You see, I was just getting ready to go out. What's this about?"

"What do you know about Margie Brown?" Officer Devers asked.

Erica started to realize there was something serious going on. "She lives here, of course. I met her about four years ago. She has an older bro ... what's up?"

"Can you tell me if she's done anything unusual? Unusual schedule? Unaccounted for time?"

"Is she in trouble?"

"Please, we just need you to answer these questions."

"Well, she's usually home when I leave for work, and she's usually home when I get home. She rarely goes out, and if she does, she never tells me where she's going. Most times when she leaves, it's just to do a load of laundry downstairs or grocery shop. What else did you want to know?"

"Who does she hang around with?"

"Well, I don't think she hangs out with the people she works with, and she doesn't socialize at the apartment complex. She goes to church with me on Sundays. She rides her bike regularly. I think she goes riding with different people, but I'm not sure who they are. I'm still new here, and we live fairly separate lives. I guess that's all I know."

"One more question. May we have a look in the apartment?"

"Do you have a search warrant?"

"We were hoping you'd just let us in."

"I have nothing to hide, but I don't feel I should just let you in. Please just leave and come back with the proper paperwork. I'll cooperate, but I don't want to be foolish."

"Of course, ma'am. Evening, ma'am. Sorry to intrude. We'll be back."

David was coming up the stairs as the officers left. "Hey, what was that all about? Are you planning a bachelorette party or something?"

"Huh? Whatever. I'm really glad you came when you did, though. They were asking me about Margie, and then they asked to search the apartment."

"Really? What do you make of it?"

"I don't know. I may not know Margie very well, but I can't imagine she's involved in anything that would involve the police. However, she was at the police station a few weeks back, so I figured I'd better answer them."

"Do you still want to go out? Would you rather stay here?"

"I think I'm more ready to go than ever. I don't want to stay here alone, not now. No, I definitely want to go."

The ride in David's red convertible was exhilarating. It was another first for Erica.

"Look," David said. "Elmer is sitting in his car over there. I can park right next to him."

"I see him now. Hey, that was one wild ride. Now my hair is such a mess. Hope you don't mind. I need to adjust your mirror to fix my hair."

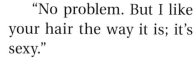

"No problem. But I like your hair the way it is; it's sexy."

"No, it's messy. There's a difference."

David shot over to the car, and after he parked, the three entered the club together. This was the first time Erica had ever gone somewhere that required a cover charge. The place was noisy, smoky, and very crowded. Soft leather loveseats surrounded the dance floor. The guys ordered the largest-size mugs of beer available, and Erica ordered a Perrier. David had already made his first move of the evening; he asked a petite brunette to dance. Erica sat on a cushy couch with Elmer and told him about the episode she had with the police.

"That's really weird, eh?" said Elmer. "So want to dance?"

"I've never danced. I don't want to embarrass you. Go ahead, you can ask someone else. I'll just wait here."

"You sure?"

"I'm fine. I just didn't want to be home tonight after that whole police ordeal."

"If you're sure." Elmer went out on the dance floor. He immediately started to move with the music and check out the opposite sex.

Moments later, a guy started hitting on Erica. She blew him off, saying she was waiting for her boyfriend. It was a half-truth. Not long after that, another guy started to talk with her and ended up sitting down with her. It was too loud to have any real conversation, so he soon left after realizing he'd get nowhere. It seemed guys in bars were much friendlier than the Christian guys she knew. Why was that? Was it just the alcohol taking effect, releasing their inhibitions? Couldn't the Holy Spirit do the same thing?

Erica noticed David talking to a girl at the bar. She was definitely the type Erica had seen him with before—tall and slender, with a slightly hard look. Erica was bothered that she hadn't seen Elmer since he first went out on the dance floor. Wondering what had happened, she went over to David to find out.

"Hi. Who's your friend?" Erica never should have asked that. David obviously didn't know the girl's name yet, and it was awkward for all. Erica then asked, "What happened to Elmer? I haven't seen him for nearly half an hour."

"Ah, he probably found himself someone and left. Don't worry, I won't leave you stranded. I'll get you a taxi if you want to leave now. I'm sorry it didn't work out for you two."

"I'm fine. Yeah, just don't leave me without notice." Erica eventually decided to go out on the dance floor to pass some time while she waited for David. She smooshed her way onto the floor and could hardly find enough space to even move her arms. It was true; a person didn't have to know how to dance at this place.

After a few minutes, she noticed a guy trying to dance

with her. He moved where she moved and mumbled something her way, but she couldn't hear what he was saying. Maybe he was singing. Then she felt his hands suddenly on every part of her body.

It took her a minute to register that she was actually being groped. She thought fast, dropped to her knees, and crawled off the overcrowded dance floor to safety. At that point, she told David she was going to sit outside. She walked out with determination in each step and tears ready to burst forth, when she spotted Elmer leaning on a car hood. She was fuming, yet suddenly confused.

"What are you doing here?" she demanded.

"The bouncer dude kicked me out."

She started to sound less hysterical, and a little more kindhearted. "Why? When?"

"Right after I split from you. When I went out on the floor with my beer mug, some dude bumped into me like he didn't even see me. I ended up spilling the beer and breaking the mug. The next thing I knew, I was being dragged out of there. I left you a message, but I take it you didn't get it."

Erica pulled her phone out of her pocket. Sure enough, a message was waiting. Erica knew she needed to be a friend to Elmer at that moment, just as much as she needed him for a friend. The talk she'd planned to have with Elmer about their relationship didn't happen that night, after all.

chapter nine

It was the Sunday after Labor Day weekend, the Sunday of the annual fall breakfast at church. After everyone got their plateful of food, the new Bible teachers presented what their Sunday Bible classes would look like. There was always so much to be learned from these seminary students. Noah was a scholar but really down-to-earth, except when he talked about his Ugeritic lexicon. He spoke with such passion, folks would more likely think he was speaking of his lover. Since he was teaching on the minor prophets, Erica nixed that one—too hard. Jared was a seminary man, as well, fulfilling his teaching requirement like the others, but he was older and had teenage kids already. His class was designed for married couples. She nixed that one, too. Mitch's class was on the book of Daniel. His introduction alone made her realize she wasn't ready for his class; his talk left her head spinning. However, it was *her* Mitch, and she would support her man by attending his class.

In an attempt to make conversation with Margie, Erica went over and asked which class she planned to take. Margie shrugged her shoulders and added, "Don't think I'll attend any of them."

The expression on Margie's face matched her demure tone. Her response almost burst Erica's bubble, but she wouldn't let it ruin her day.

To Erica's surprise, Margie actually joined the crew that went out to eat lunch. It was the first time in weeks that she had joined. Four single gals and twelve single guys. This week was a buffet week. Erica had to be careful not to eat too much. She had already gained six pounds in the last two months, and all her new clothes were getting tight.

Upon returning home around three o'clock, both Margie and Erica headed for the bedroom. It was just a one-bedroom apartment they shared. Erica was again determined to get to know Margie better.

As Margie reached for her book, Erica asked, "What's your favorite book ever?"

"I don't like to have favorites," she replied. "You?"

An unexpected continuation of dialogue occurred, yet this was just what Erica had prayed for.

"I'm not sure. I've just been reading textbooks for the past four years; I really don't know how to read for enjoyment. Can you recommend a book for me?"

"What kind of movies do you watch?"

"I'm more of a sit-com person. But I like the series *Lost*, and I used to like *Survivor*, at least the first three seasons. Actually, I don't have time to read anyway."

"Oh."

Erica was too exhausted to get another topic started, so the conversation died and so did her impetus to get to know Margie. Erica's conversing would have to be in the form of another journal entry. It was always hard to just start writing without rereading a few entries, so she went back and chose her entry from when she picked up Mitch at the airport.

September 3: Mitch looked more handsome than ever. I guess absence does make the heart grow fonder. I wish I had been with him at the wedding. It would have been such a romantic time; people would have been seeing us as a committed couple, wondering if we'd be the next ones down the aisle. From what Mitch said, they went all out; the five-course meal sounded astonishing. Three desserts served at 10 p.m. I would have died. It's such a pain being new to a job; no holidays for a year! Blasted! That's what I should have bargained for. Wonder if I could have gotten it.

While Mitch and I were eating, I kept thinking about my "situation" with you-know-who. Bottom line—there is no fixing it so I just need to go on like there is no situation. There's no way to discuss it with Mitch.

I miss Mom and Dad, especially on Sundays. I miss little Kendra. I miss being among Yankees (at least ones who aren't transplants). I miss Mom's home-cooked dinners. Lord, please, have someone from home call me. I want to hear a familiar voice.

Erica felt glum. No one ever called. She hadn't heard from family. No friends had—but then she remembered Fufe had called that past Tuesday. How could she have forgotten? They had laughed just like old times. It had been such fun to talk to someone who knew her well, who validated that she even had a history. Moving to Dallas had distanced that all from her. She had grown weary of learning new names and asking where people were from, how long they'd lived in Dallas, what they did, or how old they were. Conversations seemed so surface level, and she felt so empty. Her heart was still back with her college friends and family, but it was time for a heart transplant, and she knew it would take time. She reminded herself that God was her Constant Companion, and with a renewed spirit, she read her latest entry:

September 8–9: What a cross-cultural experience it was to spend Friday night with Jolene and Delia. Delia got real honest with me, telling me she couldn't understand how I could just move away from my family to live in a strange city on my own, just for a job. In good Mexican families, daughters stay with their parents until they marry. She really is sweet. I felt honored that she shared so personally, tears and all, about how she was married just nine months ago and that just three weeks after the wedding, her husband died. Xavier apparently had an aneurism. I can't imagine what she's been through, and at only twenty-two.

On the lighter side, I had to laugh at my own ignorance. Since I hadn't planned to spend the night at Jolene's, I, of course, had to borrow her clothes for the evening. Why I didn't have my comb with me, I'll never know, but I didn't. I won't soon forget the look on Jolene's face as she came running toward me and grabbed her comb from my hand, just as I was about to run it through my hair. She understood what I didn't: that African Americans put some kind of cream in their hair to make it shine fine, which would have ruined my porous blonde hair. I used my fingers instead.

It felt strange to not go home on Friday night, or not even call Margie, but she never lets me know whether she's going to be home or not, so I felt justified. And I guess it was the right move, as she never did ask me where I'd been. I do wonder where she thinks I was, though. Oh, well. "We're not in Kansas anymore." It actually makes me feel like I have no true home to go home to at night. I guess growing up is like that.

Margie flipped another page of her book as Erica rolled over to start her new journal entry.

chapter ten

Today had been rough for a Monday, not to mention it was the anniversary of the 9/11 attacks. Usually after a Sunday at church, Erica would have her vision restored and could handle any harassment from Roger with dignity. Oh, she would keep their relationship very professional and distant that first day back. She'd ease up and be kinder by Tuesday, knowing she'd made it through Monday. Wednesdays were usually the toughest, as she was still living off of her Sunday spiritual fix. She knew she was often looking for a compliment from Roger by then. More often than not, his compliments ended up being suggestive comments, which she'd respond to in kind or hear a sassy comeback exit her lips.

Luckily, Wednesday evening prayer groups gave her the spiritual restoration she needed to make it through the rest of the week. Sure, she seemed to be doing fine on the outside, but internally, her spirit was tension-filled and wrestling. Working in the secular world so many hours a week was like being in the Indy 500, and fellowshipping with Christians was the necessary pit stop in order to continue the race with victory.

Erica knew she had to quit her job. Although her

thoughts were a lot less holy by now, she was going to do it as a holy act of love to her Heavenly Bridegroom. She walked over to Carl Ramsey's office and leaned her head in the door.

"Can I see you for a minute?" she asked.

"For you, anything. Come on in. Sit down over here. I'll get you a drink. What would you like? I have Coke, Sprite, and spring water."

He was a large man but not fat. He looked intimidating but always seemed welcoming.

"I'm fine, thank you. I just came to talk because I realize the job here isn't a good match for me."

"Can you tell me what the problem is?"

"There's not really a problem; it just isn't a good match." She couldn't say it was sexual harassment because she knew she'd done her share to egg Roger on in recent weeks.

"You are a very sharp young lady. We've had our eye on you. We have plans for you."

With that, he reached over and rubbed her arm.

"I appreciate the encouragement, but what I need to do is quit."

"Did you get a better offer somewhere else? You owe it to us to tell us."

"No, it's not that."

"Well, let me see if I can change your mind. I happen to need a pers—, executive assistant, and I'd like for you to interview for it right now. I just need to make one call first."

"Oh, no. I'm not looking to—"

Ramsey closed the glass door behind him while Erica waited in the room, chilled from the air-conditioning, yet sweating. Her heart was racing faster than ever, yet her mind had gone into slow motion. This had to be a sleep-with-the-boss kind of job; at least, that's what everyone at work would say. After all, she'd just arrived four months ago, and now she'd be working as an executive assistant? Oh, and he seemed sleazy—a little bit, anyway. No, she had to leave. She had to get away from Roger. This would be too close. Yet she was doing a great job, and everyone told her that. Maybe this was a legitimate offer. It just seemed suspiciously coincidental. Wonder what the pay would be? Stop that! It's not an option. Ramsey finally opened the door.

"Now, let's get started. It wasn't that long ago I looked at these papers. I see you worked for Casio Electronics. Remind me of your responsibilities there."

In tears, she tried to answer the question. She finally managed to say, "I just have to leave. I'm sorry."

She left the office and then gathered her things and departed the building an hour before quitting time. She wondered if she'd ever see a check for her last two weeks of work. She didn't know what she'd do next, but she knew she did what she had to do, even if it meant giving up the opportunity of a lifetime.

She had Jolene and Delia's numbers and would call them eventually and let them know enough of what happened so they could keep rumors to a minimum. She owed them that.

chapter eleven

It had only been a few months since Erica had last found herself job hunting. On Tuesday, she went back to the agency she used before. They were a bit reluctant to work with her. Sure, they got their commission, but it may have cost them future business with her ex-company. They explained to Erica that her former company ended up paying the commission and having no one to show for it, not to mention they had done all the paperwork by then to get Erica on their payroll and on medical insurance. Erica understood their position. However, what the agency did do was offer her a position at *their* company. Erica was going to be a head-hunter. The second training session was about to begin, so she joined the other two new recruits.

The trainer was a quirky-looking, squeaky-sounding guy wearing a plaid jacket. She could tell by looking at him he'd have bad breath.

"The best place to start looking for job openings is by checking out the local newspaper," he said. "The newspaper will become your best friend. Turn with me to the death notices."

That sounded morbid to Erica.

"Here we have an executive, dead at forty-two, at a

Fortune 500 company. There is a job opening, and we need to fill it. They may promote from within to fill his position, but even if they do, it's going to mean someone else's job will be open in that company. It's your job to find the job that needs filling and match someone to it. Curtis, you can take this one. Offer our condolences, and ask them how you can assist them during this difficult time."

Erica couldn't believe what she was hearing. The man wasn't even buried yet, and they were making calls.

The trainer continued, "Look for articles about new companies starting up, new construction projects, new anything. Write these leads down for future reference if you can't use them now. Start building your files. Check and see who has recently been arrested; there may be a job opening. And when you lose the other leads, use the want ads, but remember, many positions are filled before they are even printed."

"Excuse me," interrupted Erica. "Did I just hear you correctly? Most are filled?"

"You sure did. In compliance to the law, company manuals require public posting of all job openings, but often they already have the position filled. Your job is then to call that company, not about the position being advertised but to ask if they have any other positions open. If they filled it from within, once again, there's some job left vacant that needs filling. Ask about every possibility, even entry-level positions. Keep them on the phone till you get an inside scoop, or till they hang up on you."

Erica thought it was depressing enough to try and find just one job for herself. She wasn't so sure she wanted to make a career out of finding jobs for others, but she thought she'd give it a try. The pay was minimal, but the commissions could really add up, especially if she got to place technical people in technical jobs: engineers, computer programmers, and high-powered executives.

"Miss, you have a callback on line four."

"Thanks, I'll be right on it." Erica took the call, but in the end, she felt depressed. This was just not the job for her at this point in her life. She informed her new boss that she wouldn't be returning to continue the training.

She wondered how long it would be before she told Margie or Mitch or anyone else that she had quit her job downtown. Since she didn't want to job hunt and didn't want to go home, she went to the movie theater to kill some time and settle her mind. She watched a 1:45 matinee at a theater just around the corner. Upon leaving the theater, the only thing she could remember about the whole movie was the laughter that constantly erupted from others. Her mind had been elsewhere, and so had her ability to laugh.

chapter twelve

When the September rent came due, Margie learned the truth. Erica finally confessed. "I am a few bucks short on my half of the rent. I guess you need to know why; I quit my job."

"I figured something was up. Why did you quit?"

"Long story."

"When did you quit?"

"Two weeks ago. I was looking for a new job until just three days ago. My ego just couldn't take any more rejection, so for the past three days, I've just been vegging at home and reading a book from your shelf. It's been really good too. Friesen's book *Decision Making and the Will of God*."

"I haven't read it. It's from a box of books my mom gave me last year when she moved. So you liked it, eh?"

"It was just what I needed to deal with the transition. Next time, I need to choose a job more carefully and not jump in so quickly. I made a big mistake last time."

"So you didn't like the job?"

"I had some problems with my boss, problems I don't want to repeat."

"Problems you don't want to talk about?"

"Kind of a sexual harassment thing, but not quite."

Her comment didn't surprise Margie.

"I'll pay the rent until you get a job. But get some temp work to help out with food and bills, okay?"

"Wow, that's super generous of you. I can't believe you'd do that for me."

"No problem. I have a great job designing houses. You need one, too."

Margie realized her roommate needed help, and she was willing to do something for her. Sure, Erica could be confusing to Margie, and her actions sometimes annoyed her, but Margie knew it was she who had invited Erica to move down to Dallas; she felt some responsibility to help her. Margie had been paying the rent by herself for two years now, so for her, it just meant postponing a car purchase a little longer.

The next person to find out was Mitch. Erica felt guilty for not telling him earlier, but he was so busy with classes, it had never really come up. They hadn't seen each other except at church the past two weeks, and there were always people around. She was putting off the inevitable in hopes of being able to tell him about her new job as kind of a happy-ending surprise to a good news/bad news story. Too bad there was no good news to tell.

"Sweetie, I can't believe you didn't tell me you quit your job." Mitch sounded faintly condescending. "It makes me question what we have going here. You just went through a big deal, and yet you didn't confide in me. I can't believe it, Erica."

She could tell he was seething but trying to cover up his anger. She was speechless, and Mitch was still talking.

"I feel hurt. I need to hang up before I say something I'll regret. I'll call you later—or tomorrow."

Erica wished she hadn't told him over the phone. How stupid of her. Could anything else go wrong? She knew he still cared about her, but she had a nagging doubt building up in her. Would he be angry enough at her to ditch her? No, he was bigger than that. He just needed time to cool off, or so she hoped. At least he hadn't said anything really mean, right?

Erica busied herself with straightening some piles of magazines and grouping her nail polish bottles by pinks, reds, purples, and oranges. She tossed the green polish that she had only used once and wiped her makeup containers down so they looked brand new again. Next, she started emptying out the closet, putting all her clothes on her bed. How would she organize it this time? Sleeveless to long sleeve didn't matter anymore in her one-season city of hot and hotter. Should she go for solids in one section and prints in another? Or put things in matching sets, ready to wear? This time, she'd arrange it all by colors— all the blacks, then browns, the purples and blues, then the greens, darker shades first, and finally the yellows, oranges, and reds, working from lighter to darker shades. She continued arranging her clothes till she put the last piece back in her closet. She collapsed on her bed, satisfied with her accomplishment.

Elmer came by to see why she wasn't by the pool yet for their usual evening swim. She told him she needed to skip swimming tonight. Elmer indicated with his puppy dog eyes he'd miss her but left without argument.

Erica showered and realized she hadn't eaten all day. She was proud of herself and decided not to eat then, either. She turned on the TV but fell asleep waiting for Mitch's call.

chapter thirteen

The next Sunday, there was a new face in the crowd. Gabriella was her name. She had just moved down from Ohio and was looking for a good church. She seemed so happy-go-lucky and wore her auburn hair in pigtails. Erica invited her to join the singles for lunch. Later, Gabriella came over to the apartment to continue talking. They hit it off right away. Gabriella was a stockbroker, but she seemed so unassuming despite landing such a highfalutin job. The hours passed by quickly as they got to know each other. It was 4:30 p.m. when Erica was walking Gabriella to her car and they saw Elmer.

"Hey Elmer, come meet my new friend, Gabriella."

"Pleased to meet you, my lady." He took her hand and gave it a peck.

"Frankly, I love this Southern hospitality," Gabriella said with a sweet giggle.

The three of them chatted away, and everything was fine until Gabriella mentioned Erica being out of work. Elmer turned his head, raised his eyebrows, and opened his eyes real big, flashing a look of disbelief her way.

"Out of work? You? Since when?"

"I'm sorry, Elmer. I've just been too embarrassed to tell

anyone I quit my job. Too many questions I didn't want to answer. I was hoping to find work quickly, but I haven't."

"You don't have any money, do you?"

"Not really, but Margie offered to pay the rent, and if I get a few temp jobs, I can hopefully keep up with the other bills and food."

"I can help with the food. I get all them dented cans from work real cheap. You come over and just pick what you want."

"Oh, that's great. I'd want to pay you for them, of course."

"A buck a bag, and then they're yours."

"Wow! I can't believe how great everyone's being. It's starting to feel like I have this big huge family down here."

Gabriella finally chimed in. "I need to get going. Thanks for the wonderful day. I'll be back at church next week."

She gave Erica a look that said that she might just have found the church she was looking for.

"Nice meeting you, fine lady. Come around again." Elmer had a way of making women feel special.

"Nice meeting you too. And I'll be praying that you get the right job, and soon, Erica."

"Thanks, Gabriella."

Elmer and Erica watched as Gabriella drove off in her beat-up old Honda. Erica was thinking she may have just met a new best friend.

Elmer and Erica continued talking in his apartment after she filled two bags with groceries. He was so sweet, but she continued in her resolve that they remain just friends. She invited him to come along to church the next week, but he declined because he didn't have nice clothes to wear.

"Ridiculous. People can wear jeans and T-shirts to our church. You'll look fine." Erica breathed a prayer for Elmer.

"You know Sunday is my only day to sleep in."

"Tell you what. You go to church with me, and I'll go out to that rodeo you've been bugging me about. Not a date, of course. Deal?"

"You drive a tough bargain, lady. I'll think about it."

Erica knew it was a sly move, but she also knew that Elmer needed Jesus, and if this worked, why not?

chapter fourteen

Erica needed a week that would pass by uneventfully, but that just couldn't happen. Erica grabbed her phone. "Hello?"

"Is this Erica?"

"Aaah—yes. Who's this?" The voice sounded familiar, but she couldn't place it.

"I miss our talks on the bus."

Her heart sank. Oh, no. Could it be? "Roger?"

"So you *do* remember."

"How'd you get my number? I'm not listed."

"I checked your files—you were only an excuse away. I just told Carl that I needed to ask you about one of the accounts you had worked on. Not too difficult."

"How's everything at work? I miss Jolene and Delia."

"The usual, except Josie got fired. No real news on Jolene or Delia. And I decided I'm going to stick it out. I've been getting some good leads and assignments. So, where are you working?"

"I'm still looking for the right job. Doing temp work a couple days a week. So what is it you needed help with? An account I worked on?"

"Well, it's more like I have a proposal for you to

consider regarding one of our accounts. I have to go to Houston October 19 on business. I thought if you weren't too busy, you could join me. Otherwise, it will be a very long, lonely drive all by myself. The work part shouldn't keep me too busy, and we could enjoy the nightlife there. What do you say?"

"I say, 'What would your wife think?'"

"You know she can't go; she's got to stay home with the kids."

"That's not what I meant, and you know it."

Ignoring her, he continued, "You must know I miss your company. Come along, indulge me, and make my trip bearable. All expenses paid. No strings attached. Live it up a little. You in?"

"No way. I thought when I left the company, you'd be gone from my life. Let's keep it that way. No more calls."

"You don't know what you're missing. Here, take down my number. You might just change your mind. It's ..."

"I don't need your number." Erica slammed the phone down so hard it bounced back off the cradle; she could still hear Roger talking. She then carefully placed the phone back, making sure it was turned off. The nerve of him. Now that he had her number, there would be no such thing as fleeing temptation. It would just come and find her. And it's not like *he* didn't know why she had quit her job.

Roger was rather handsome, was successful at work, had a wife and kids, so what was he missing? What was he looking for? Adventure? Was his life too mundane? Did he thrive on risk? Was it just that she was so alluring to him, he couldn't control himself and lost all sense? Her background in psychology made her want to know, but her Christian morals kept her from seeking answers.

chapter fifteen

Wednesday night finally came. Together, Margie and Erica had cleaned the house so it would be spic-and-span for company. Their small group was coming over for dessert and prayer, and Margie was busy getting her devotional ready. Everyone arrived on time or early. Drinks were served: three Cokes, two ice teas, and two waters. It was an Indian summer night, and as usual, they didn't turn on the A/C. Sweat oozed and dripped from the guests; it would probably be the last time they came over.

When it was time to share requests, Erica mentioned she might be moving; she had been talking with Mike from the efficiency apartment downstairs, who wanted to sublet it by the end of October.

"The great thing about his apartment is the A/C is free since it's on the same meter as the office of the manager, and the rent is less than half the cost of this apartment. But as you know, my big obstacle is that I still need a job so I can afford it. He wants me to move in as soon as possible."

Margie knew Erica had been talking with Mike, so this news was no surprise. However, when she began to pray, everyone was surprised.

"Lord, help Erica to make the right decision about

whether to move in with Mike or not. Give her counsel and wisdom and keep her from harm."

It seemed to Erica that Margie's prayer would never end. What was she thinking? Erica wasn't going to move in with Mike. As soon as the prayer time was over, Erica sought the floor.

"I want to clarify something. There's no way I'm moving in with Mike. He's moving out and into a house he just bought, but he still has four months left on his contract here. To sublet means to take over a contract. That's all I'm considering."

Everyone nodded and assured her that they had understood her intentions. It still left her feeling uncomfortable, remembering how her own roommate had prayed, but at least it showed concern.

After everyone left, Erica sat down with Margie and told her how uncomfortable she felt about the prayer. It was their first real conversation in five months.

Margie got squared away and then added, "I hope you'll stay. I don't feel safe living alone."

That statement stunned Erica. Margie had been living alone for two years. Why would she suddenly feel like she needed a roommate? If anyone could handle life alone, it was Margie. She could fix her own car and could handle the repairs in the apartment. She could grow her nails or design a building that could withstand a tornado. She could do anything. Erica asked her to explain.

Fidgeting and looking more uptight, Margie cleared her throat and continued, "I guess I should tell you something. Do you remember the night I said I was at the police station, back in June?"

"Yeah. You didn't want to talk about it, I figured."

"No, I didn't. I—just let me start at the beginning."

"I'm listening."

"I was contacted by my boss the day before. He told me I didn't need to come into work the next day. Instead, he needed a favor. He said he had a distant cousin visiting from Europe. The cousin wanted to tour Dallas. My boss couldn't do it himself. So he asked me to do it. I figured I had better say yes. I even thought it'd be fun. Anyway, I wasn't too busy at work."

"Did he pay you extra to show her around?"

"Him. Show *him* around. Yeah, a little. I took him to the usual stuff. Then I rented a tandem bike so we could enjoy the lake."

"That was a creative idea. Did he like that?"

"I don't know how to answer that." Her words suddenly came out much slower and much more serious as she spoke. "We had gone a few miles when we stopped for a rest. It was starting to get dark by then. I was still in business mode. I was thinking of him as a client I needed to entertain, not as a relative of my boss. I hadn't realized how different this situation really was compared to the others. On that day, I was playing tour guide to a tourist, to someone seeking to discover whatever he could about America and Americans. The next thing I knew, he threw himself on me and ripped open my blouse, and then he forced me …"

By now, she was crying. Erica had never seen Margie cry.

"I'm so sorry. Here, try and catch your breath."

Margie was finally calming down.

"Is that why you ended up at the police station?"

"I tried to file a report," Margie explained, "but I was told that it was difficult to do anything about the situation under normal circumstances. And nearly impossible to do anything since he was a foreigner."

"I'm so sorry. Is that why some policemen came around asking about you?"

"Huh? What policemen?"

"Labor Day weekend, two policemen came by, asking about you: who your friends were, how you spent your time. I wasn't very helpful since I knew so little about you. Then they asked to come in and look around, but I felt funny about it, so I didn't let them in. Did you ever end up talking to them?"

"I have no idea why they would ask about me, and no, I never talked to any policemen." Margie turned the conversation back to where it all started. "Can you at least see why I might want someone to live with me? Erica, please stay. I know I prayed for God's guidance in your life, but that doesn't mean I can't share my opinion, does it?"

"If I stay, can we keep talking like we're doing now? I need people in my life I can talk to and tell about my day and who care where I go. Can you offer that? I know I'm asking a lot."

"I guess I've just lived alone for so long, I've gotten too independent. If you'll stay, I'll try."

Erica had her answer. She suddenly had two female friends: Margie and Gabriella. Now all she needed was a job.

chapter sixteen

Mitch had finished up the first half of his teaching
series on Daniel and was ready for some fun with Erica.

He knew he wanted to
spend some alone time with
her that Sunday afternoon,
so he convinced her to ditch
the singles' group and go
out to lunch alone with him
instead. They found a deli
and bought a pastrami and
rye sandwich, a BLT sub,
apples, grapes, some egg
salad, and a slice of Dutch
apple cheesecake. Erica pulled a Perrier and two Starbucks
cappuccinos from the store's cooler. They put all the food
into a basket in the back of Mitch's car and drove around
till they found a beautiful, secluded spot in Carrollton for
their picnic. Mitch carried the thick, blue comforter and
the drink bag while Erica carried the basket. The afternoon
was sweetly romantic. She just enjoyed looking into
Mitch's steel-blue eyes; it seemed like the perfect

opportunity for him to lean in and kiss her. She could sense it was coming.

"Erica, we've been growing closer together these past five months. I've enjoyed my job more and been a better student and a better person because of you. You have put an extra bounce of joy in each step I take." Erica took it all in until her dream world was cut short by Mitch's query: "I want to know how you feel about me."

She had been sort of expecting this but still said, "Oh, Mitch. I'm just not real smooth at expressing my feelings on the spot like this. But I'll give it a try. Let's see. I know I always look forward to seeing you each week, and I've really enjoyed your class on Daniel. Your teaching is so refreshing. You've helped keep me steady and strong, and given me hope. Okay, that's like the stuff I tell my mom when she asks about us. Now, for the important stuff." Erica got real playful and flirty in her voice. "I find you cute and adorable, and I love looking into your eyes. I love holding your hand, especially when we try to hide the fact." Erica got back to being more serious again. "I guess I haven't even begun to see an end in our relationship, so this slow-and-steady pace seems to be working for us." She paused. "What else would you like to know?"

"That was good. Real good." Mitch's face was beaming after her encouraging words. He shifted his position to get a little closer to Erica. "I have something I'd like to ask you, but please don't put more weight into this question than intended. I just want to know your thoughts." He coughed. "Do you think you'd want to marry a guy who is going to be a pastor?"

"Well, when I was in college, people would ask me what my major was, and I could handle that. But when they asked me what I wanted to do with my life, I would really struggle. I felt two callings on my life. One was to be a mom, and the other was to be a pastor's wife. I honestly feel it's a special calling, and I have felt it was mine."

"That's incredible."

Erica continued, "I would daydream about having an inner city ministry, with homeless people ringing our doorbell at 2 a.m., and my pastor husband and I would invite them in. Then we'd end up helping these guys get sober, share how Jesus could make a difference in their lives, and keep in touch with them, maybe even have the church help one of them through seminary. Do you think I'm really wacko?"

"Well, that's quite a dream, and a cool one at that. Mine is more like I am this awe-inspiring preacher, church of seven thousand people, and the church has a really strong missions program, causing change around the world because the congregation loves God so much and wants to see the world reached as their number one priority."

"Well then, I have a question for you, mister: what do you want in a wife?"

"That's easy. Someone I can cherish. Someone I can share my heart and life with. Someone to save me from the utter loneliness of the single life. And someone who likes to spend their free time like I do."

Mitch and Erica continued to talk and enjoy the day. It actually started to get cool, so they packed up and headed home. There was no kiss, but there was a lot of desire and respect developing between the couple.

chapter seventeen

Job hunting all week had drained Erica of her energy, her leads, and her hope. Roger's offer of Houston was starting to sound a whole lot more appealing with each thought she allowed. With her ego at an all-time low, she figured she needed some way to treat herself. Roger had never actually said he was expecting her to be a fling or anything; maybe he really was just looking for company—after all, Houston would be a nice place, and it's always more fun to share experiences than to just have them alone. Sure, he should go with his wife, but his wife wasn't available. Erica was unemployed, available, and an honorable girl who might actually keep Roger from doing something foolish. Maybe she should take advantage of his offer. It'd be fun. But what would she tell Margie, now that they were talking and all?

Erica had about two hours to find Roger. She looked up his address, Googled it, packed a bag, and drove over to his house. It took about seven minutes to get there, but all she found was a house with an open garage, no car, and two pink tricycles on the lawn. He had already gone. Her stomach felt sick, but she was happy about one thing: she wouldn't have to come up with a lie for Margie; she was going back to her own apartment that night.

Who was she kidding? If Mitch knew what she was capable of considering, he'd dump her into a landfill and leave her there. She knew she couldn't live with this constant internal war of inconsistency in her life. She was glad to be home. She stood, looking out her window and prayed:

"Dear God, I'm losing it. I'm not being the person I want to be. I can't believe what I considered doing! I'm no dummy. I remember when I was a teen—even then I couldn't get away with doing stupid stuff 'cause I knew better. I knew what was right and wrong then, and now I struggle at every turn to do right. Be my strength. I feel so unprepared for the things that get thrown at me in this adult world. I need help. In Jesus's name, Amen."

She sat down on the couch and opened her Bible. Right then, Margie walked in. Erica's Bible sat open as they talked. Erica closed her unread Bible an hour later and went to bed. She had missed yet another time in the Word.

chapter eighteen

Brrrring. *Brr…* "Hello."

"Is Erica Webb there?"

"Yeah, that's me."

"It's Estelle. I'm sorry to bother you so early, but I have a temp job I thought you'd be interested in. A nationally known chip-producing company needs some extras to help with inventory. The pay isn't what you were looking for, but it'll include lunch and dinner, and you're guaranteed pay for twelve hours, so I thought I'd run it by you. They'll need you by eight o'clock. Does this sound like a job for you?"

"Sure, I can do it. Beats spending another day of doing data entry and answering phones. Give me the details."

Erica got dressed and drove off, picking up an Egg McMuffin and an orange juice on the way. Her favorite job the week before had been her three-day gig at the country club—free Coke, free buffet lunch, and easy hours. It was a real treat after being cooped up in the damp basement of an old apartment complex answering the phone and listening to tenant complaints all day. She wondered what the people at this place would be like.

Erica arrived at the office at 8:15 a.m.

"You Erica? Next floor. Ask for Betty."

The receptionist at least let Erica know she was at the right place, but her mechanical demeanor made her feel like a piece of meat. Erica's ego was still fragile, and her sensitivity quotient was climbing steadily. She rode in the elevator with several others. *Ding.* She got off. The first two hours of counting boxes of chips seemed like an eternity. The first break was at ten o'clock. Erica was ushered to a room with the others who had been hired for the day.

At 10:15, someone came and asked her to work with a different team, since they were falling behind. This portion of the day flew by; the other two temps were talkative and joked around (no wonder they were behind). Erica wished work could be this fun every day. For lunch, the company had pizza delivered, and for dinner, they ordered gourmet subs. There was plenty of food for everyone, and lots left over. Erica secretly wished she could have taken all the extra food home.

chapter nineteen

The next day, Erica called on some leads, e-mailed her resume to a few places, and prayed someone would invite her out for lunch. Around eleven o'clock, she heard a knock on her door. She opened the door and saw Gabriella standing there.

"Glad you're home," she said. "Have you eaten yet?"

Erica's heart jumped, and she whispered a silent *Thank you* toward heaven. "No. What did you have in mind?"

"I have a hankering for Mexican and a voucher for fifty dollars. Want to join me? My treat."

"You bet. Did you know you are an answer to prayer? I just prayed someone would invite me out for lunch."

"That's just like Him."

Lunch was filling, but they still had room for a latte. It was four o'clock before they knew it.

"Erica, this will probably be the only time our schedules allow us to enjoy a lunch out, as you'll have a job real soon."

Erica hoped her friend's words would prove to be prophetic. "Thanks, Gabriella. To think, we only met a few weeks ago, and you're already such a special friend. I've needed someone like you to talk things out with."

"Erica?" She immediately recognized the man's voice, just as a hand landed on her shoulder from behind. She turned around. It was Roger. Her two worlds were about to collide.

"Oh, hi, Roger. You just arrive?" Erica was in the mood to enjoy the moment.

"Actually, I just finished eating. I was sitting in the booth behind you two. I kept wondering if it was you. So who's your friend?"

"Oh, forgive me. Roger, this is Gabriella. She just moved down to Dallas last month. She had today off, and I'm still unemployed, so she took me out. Guess you had the day off as well, eh?"

"Technically we had the day off, but I still worked this morning. Then I joined a friend for lunch. She's using the restroom."

"Some things never change."

Erica wondered what his relationship was like with this female friend. It was a dig she should not have made if she was going to treat Roger with Christian kindness. Plus, she could tell something had registered with Gabriella. She immediately regretted it.

After they parted company with Roger, Erica filled Gabriella in on a few details. She explained that they used to work together and he just didn't seem to respect her boundaries. She hadn't told anyone about Roger and didn't expect to start now. Actually, she didn't find him very attractive this particular day. Erica usually got into guys wearing jeans and a T-shirt, but that look didn't work for Roger. He was definitely a suit-and-tie guy. Erica had tried unsuccessfully to forget Roger, but she knew if he popped into her mind again, she'd try and think of this jeans and T-shirt version of him, not her previous image of a debonair man ready to whisk her off at a moment's notice. Erica wanted to do the right thing, but she kept finding the wrong thing so attractive and so available.

chapter twenty

Margie was cleaning up the kitchen when Erica came in to make a snack. "Erica, could you do me a favor?"

"Sure, I have time to clean; what's up?"

"Not that kind of favor. Have a seat and hear me out. I can grab something for you while we talk. Granola suit you?"

"Sure." Erica was now a tad bit curious.

Margie continued, "Here's the deal. I've been getting to know a guy who does business with my company. We e-mail and talk on the phone almost every day. Well, a few months ago, Wally tried to witness to me. That's when I discovered he was a Christian. I, of course, try to keep business business, but that doesn't always happen. I ended up telling him I was already a Christian, and then we started talking about his new, growing faith, mixed with the usual business stuff. Long story short: He brought up the topic of dating. He said he wanted to know what is expected when a Christian guy dates a Christian girl. I know you're in a relationship with Mitch, but Wally's just looking to do some research on dating the Christian way. He just wants to have one date, that's all. I was wondering if I could give him your name. I'd do it, but I need to keep our relationship strictly professional."

"I guess I could do that for you—for him—whatever. I need to talk it over with Mitch, though. I wouldn't want him to get the wrong impression. I think he's pretty understanding about these things, going into the ministry and all."

"That's great, and Wally will really appreciate it. I'll tell him it's okay to call you, then? And don't worry; Mitch will understand."

"Should I tell him now or wait to be sure Wally's going to call?"

"Whatever you think. Personally, I wouldn't even bother telling Mitch anything."

"It's not a bother. Besides, Mitch made me promise total honesty and total communication after the quitting-my-job incident. I owe him that much."

"I see. Guess you do. You don't have to do this date thing, you know. I can find someone else."

"I know. But you asked me for a reason, and I feel I may have something to offer him. I've been doing a lot of thinking about the whole dating thing recently."

Erica decided to call Mitch right away. She usually waited for him to call her; it just made their relationship work better, but she really needed to make sure he was informed in a timely manner.

His voice sounded particularly deep and romantic over the phone. "Erica, to what do I owe this unexpected pleasure?"

"Oh, I just wanted to hear your voice." She was chickening out. How do you go from, "To what do I owe this unexpected pleasure?" to bringing up you're going to go out with a guy you've never met? She told him she was going to do something unusual as a favor to Margie, but she secretly hoped he wouldn't follow up on it.

"You're a fun girl, Erica. Hey, I'm glad you and Margie are getting along so well. Miracles do happen. Love ya."

Did he just say what she thought he said? She wasn't sure, but she knew it wasn't the time to ask him to repeat it. She ended their conversation with words she trusted would be true for her as well: "Pleasant dreams."

After she hung up the phone, she ran right over to her journal to mark December 2 as the day he may have said, "Love ya."

chapter twenty-one

He stood at the open door in his beige tweed sports coat, clenching a rose between his teeth. The moment could have come across like a corny scene in a B-movie, but it didn't play out that way at all; Erica had just been swept off her feet. This guy was drop-dead gorgeous. He was shorter than she expected—a mere five feet, ten inches; however, his wispy blond hair and dark tan accented his dimples and adorable grin, and his bass voice beautifully articulated the words, "Are *you* my date for this evening?" And his pecs looked great, from what she could see.

Erica was trying to remember if she had gotten this date through winning a lottery drawing or if she had handpicked him from a catalogue. She was speechless. She could tell Margie was peeking out from the kitchen. Erica couldn't believe her roommate had set this up for her.

"Yes, yes, I'm your date." She didn't hide her excitement very well.

"This rose is a token of my hope for a perfect evening with a lovely Christian lady like yourself. The red petals remind me of Christ's blood that has cleansed me from my past, and the thorns remind me of the pain He endured so my life can now have a new start. Miss Erica, please find this single rose some living water, and we can be off."

Okay, now Erica was getting it. Perfect guy, overly zealous new Christian: it was going to be a long night.

After a few minutes, she said, "You know, Wally, I'm just an average gal. I'm a Christian, and I love Jesus, but I don't talk about Him all the time like you do. I don't feel I need to, I guess."

Erica continued talking for another minute when Wally interrupted. "I'm so relieved. You see, I have a really raunchy background. After I became a Christian, I really changed. The problem is, I've been struggling these past two months because I *really* like women, but I've been afraid I wouldn't know how to handle a Christian woman or relationship— or even know what to do. I'm used to hopping into bed with someone on the first date. I figured if I talked Christian, it'd help get me through this first date without the usual sex. I don't really know what to do on a date otherwise."

"Oh, just be yourself," Erica said. "The idea of a first date is to get to know each other better, that's all. Start with a few compliments, a few questions, and don't be afraid of a little silence. I should talk."

"It sounds easy enough, but you can't believe how nervous I've been all day."

Erica enjoyed the evening at the Mexican restaurant; getting Wally was pure delight. Wally and Erica continued talking about their common faith, but in deep and meaningful ways, not the overwhelming yet superficial way things started out. Of course, Wally had just begun to get the picture, so they planned to get together for another training session.

chapter twenty-two

Christmas events just snuck up on Erica. There had been parties to attend and lots of church-sponsored events in town. Tonight, she would be attending a choir performance of *The Messiah* with Mitch, Gabriella, and her boyfriend Johannes, and later, they'd drive through the Nights of Lights display. The best part was, she had received her first paycheck earlier that day. Finally, after months of unemployment, Erica had started a job at the firm where Gabriella worked. It wasn't the dream job she had been hoping for, but it would get her away from job-hunting, and that had sounded like the best form of peace on earth she could imagine.

Erica had tried out her negotiating skills during that job interview. She managed to get a dollar an hour over what they were offering, and they made allowance for her to visit her family over the holidays, as planned. Erica was so thankful her parents had paid for her to be home for the holidays; however, she felt terrible about the cost of the last-minute ticket.

chapter twenty-three

Wally and Erica had scheduled two additional times to get together, December 16 and 22. Mitch had already left for his home in New York, so she still hadn't told him about Wally. She knew Margie had her suspicions, but since Margie had gotten her involved with Wally, she hoped she'd play dumb and mind her own business.

The truth was, Erica simply couldn't resist Wally's charm and transparent honesty. His worldly life experience seemed to add to his magnetism. Although quite premature for any relationship, Wally had found out that, yes, Christian girls really did know how to kiss, and yes, they really, really liked doing it. So when he asked her out for New Year's Eve (after she got back from New Jersey), she knew it would be for a real date, and there was no way to deny it. She knew she needed to clean up the messy situation she had created but lacked the will to do it. She wanted to be with Wally. And she wanted to be with Mitch. And she wanted to serve God.

Erica couldn't open her Bible these days without conviction piercing her heart. She couldn't stand to pray one more time to ask forgiveness for something she knew she'd want to do the next time the opportunity presented itself. After all, she could have fun when she didn't let her heart communicate with her mind. And she didn't seem to care about what she was doing, but she cared enough to ask God to help her to care again.

chapter twenty-four

It was quite early to be up on a Saturday, and Erica had already eaten breakfast and finished packing for her trip to New Jersey. It was also Mitch's twenty-third birthday, but her mind wasn't on him right then. She had other things think about. She sat down in her living room and asked God if non-Christians' lives were any different than hers.

God, what is it really like to live without a desire to serve You? What would life be like without rules or standards of right and wrong? Show me what's worth holding on to; what, if anything, would make Christianity seem great, and not just seem like a mundane killjoy. I want to know what life would be like without You hampering it. I don't like always feeling restrained and repressed. I want some freedom. I need …

In a flash, it was as if Erica had been captured and taken to another realm of existence. At first, all was pitch-black; she felt eerie, and shivers ran up and down her body. Next, the blackness mixed with red and started to swirl around her. She couldn't breathe normally. She was feeling naked and cold and frightened to the core as she envisioned her soul being squeezed right out from her chest. She shook uncontrollably as flashes of evil sights pierced the scene. Now she was gasping for breath.

Erica was shivering, for it seemed as if Satan himself had come for a visit. She tried to reason in the midst of this virtual reality. Was this what life would be like without God's presence? Was this what the Holy Spirit kept her from feeling? Did people who had played into Satan's hands experience things like this? She took what was left of her mind and begged God to remove the horrific scene. Again, her God was faithful to the request.

Instantly, Erica was released from those few seconds of life in a demonic black hole, and she now experienced an indescribable peace. She praised God for making things so clear, but she still didn't take time to humble herself and confess her sin. She needed to get to the airport.

In just a few hours, Erica's plane would be taking her to her family back East. How could she go from the most profound spiritual experience she'd had since her conversion in third grade to light-hearted socializing with family? How could she keep the sanctity of the holiday, celebrating her Savior's birth, in light of her behavior and inappropriate desires? It was a drama she couldn't mentally rehearse since she, too, was unable to foresee how it would play out.

While trying to get comfortable on an uncomfortable plastic airport chair, Erica overheard a lady talking hysterically. It seemed she had cornered the attention of a stranger. Erica listened in:

"I'm on the last leg of my journey home—if you can call it that anymore. I just came from a memorial service for my son in Korea." She couldn't control her weeping. "He was only twenty years old. He was on a practice flight in a helicopter that malfunctioned. It was only last year I buried my husband, who fell off our roof. Now I have no one at home and no one to ever return back home."

Erica peeked around to see who was talking. She looked like a wreck: frazzled hair, baggy eyes, no makeup, and torn, dirty clothing. She had apparently been taking advantage of her free international flight drinks, as well. Erica wanted to butt in and share with her the hope that Christ could bring, but it seemed too late to assuage this woman's immediate needs. Erica felt she couldn't say anything without speaking from a lie. Her theology hadn't been matching up with her actions. She'd been a hypocrite who didn't want to be one, but now, seeing someone who really needed Jesus, she wished she had handled things differently with Wally and Mitch. It made sense to her that if she would focus on the lost world around her, it could give her the impetus to live a holy life. After all, others needed to know the love and forgiveness she knew. Oh, how could she be so unkind, so unfair, so dishonest with those so close to her?

Erica had been through every emotion already today, and now she was about to land in Newark. She had slept most of the flight, hoping to rejuvenate her impoverished soul and bolster her fragile emotional state. When she opened her eyes, it was already dark. She peered out the window. The city lights seemed to electrify not only the city but also her spirit. She felt a tinge of joy as she imagined seeing her family and the familiar Christmas lights.

She soon felt the plane descending while noticing her own spirit soaring. She was experiencing a wave of peace on earth falling on her once again. *Shalom.*

To her relief, she spotted her father right away. They quickly got through baggage claim and were soon on their way to her childhood home.

chapter twenty-five

Erica's sister, Sherilyn, and the rest of her family came over to celebrate Christmas Eve after their church service. Everyone enjoyed the scrumptious roast lamb and mashed potatoes at Mom and Dad's house. The day was full of engaging conversation with family and catching up with all the fast-growing nieces and nephews. Erica's heart was full, and so was her stomach. She sat at the table, silently seduced by the buzz of conversation as she sipped her coffee, wondering when she'd have her own little ones to share Christmases with her.

Her family was Norwegian and she grew up following many Scandinavian Christmas traditions. She enjoyed making Norwegian cookies made with presses and forms and even some deep fried cookies. She loved the tradition of opening presents on Christmas Eve (versus Christmas Day). Of course, she opened stockings from Santa on Christmas morning, like everyone else. She usually attacked hers before anyone else was awake. Her father had discouraged the use of lighting candles on the trees, as he recounted the many times during his childhood in Norway when a fiery tree had been rushed out of neighboring houses.

Typically, there was a package or two to open later on Christmas Day, but the big family celebration was the night before. Christmas Day was always considered a more sacred day, as her family attended a special ten o'clock service at her church. She remembered how she would go to church and meet up with all her friends, who were anxious to go home and finally open gifts. She relished in the fact that she had already opened her gifts.

Her attention focused again on her little nieces and nephews. Would they share her childhood frustration of having to wait to open presents? She figured the next hour would seem like an eternity for them. She knew the routine: clear the table, rinse the dishes, fill the dishwasher, put away all the food, and wipe down the kitchen counters and table, then finally open presents.

After Erica had finished wiping off the counters, she retired to a couch in the den, where the guys were watching football or catching a nap. The warmth in the fireplace brought forth yet more memories of Christmases past—memories of setting up the tree, finding that elusive decoration "in a box somewhere," taking a break to eat cookies and drink cocoa on a full stomach, and eventually going to sleep and hoping Mom and Dad wouldn't forget to fill the stockings. They never did forget.

Sherilyn interrupted Erica's recollections. "You have a phone call. Who's *Mitch*?"

Erica grabbed the phone from Sherilyn's teasing hold. Trying to sound calm, she simply said, "Hello?"

"Merry Christmas, Sweet One."

Mitch's call brought Erica back to life. She began talking a mile a minute. "Hi, hi. Merry Christmas to you, too. And happy birthday. It's so good to hear your voice. What have you been doing? I can't believe we've been missing each other's calls all week."

"I know. I'm so miserable. It's great being with my family and all, but they are getting sick and tired of hearing about you all the time. They all want to meet you. They're planning to come visit us in Dallas over Easter. You can meet them then."

"Super, but I wish I could have met them now; I would have loved to. Tell them that. I just couldn't work it out with my job. At least I was able to have two days with my family."

The conversation started to get more personal as Erica continued walking to a more private location. She envied those people who were able to be with their special loved one *and* their family during this special holiday time. Why did she have to choose?

Erica's mom called from the hallway, "Erica, it's time for gifts; get off the phone and join us."

"Okay, Mom. Be right there." That's what came out, but she wanted to say, "Are you crazy? Not now. I finally have my Mitch, and I want to keep him." She was really enjoying her long-awaited chat. "Mitch, hearing from you has been so wonderful, but I have to go now. Wish your family a Merry Christmas for me."

"Merry Christmas to you, Erica. Greet your family from me."

The gift opening was always a highlight. It always started out slowly and orderly but soon turned into utter chaos, and when things were winding to a close, Dad would present his girls with a special gift that he had purchased for them himself.

Once all the gifts had been exchanged, Sherilyn couldn't wait any longer to ask more about Mitch. She quickly piled up her gifts and her husband's gifts and all the gifts the children had opened. Then she sent the kids off to get ready for their special Christmas Eve sleepover at Grandma's house so she could start her interrogation. Sherilyn interrogated Erica on her love life. Erica was tired but eager to talk to someone about Mitch. She wasn't ready to say that he was the one, but she indicated that the relationship was worth pursuing.

She found talking about Mitch to be therapeutic. She knew she needed to process more about her situation with Wally, but she couldn't do it with Sherilyn. She knew she still had a New Year's Eve date scheduled with Wally, but she justified it. She didn't want to be alone for New Year's, and Mitch would still be gone. She hated her double life, but she didn't want to do what was necessary to fix it.

As she lay on her bed, trying to fall asleep, she reflected on the baby born in Bethlehem, the one who could love her even now, even in her depravity. She pondered that kind of love.

chapter twenty-six

New Year's arrived, and so did Wally—right to Erica's Texas doorstep. He drove up in his Dodge RAM pickup at nine o'clock to take her out for dinner.

Wally had reserved a special table for two in a secluded corner of the restaurant. It was cozy, and the lighting set the mood to over-the-top romantic. They celebrated with an expensive bottle of wine that Wally picked out for their dinner, but he also ordered a few Jack Daniel's for himself. Erica just sipped the wine throughout dinner and probably managed to drink three glassfuls before they left.

After dinner, Wally and Erica walked hand-in-hand over to Shooters to play some pool. A gust of wind almost knocked her over, or so she thought. She was feeling more than tipsy. They tried out the billiard table. It was fun to play pool all dressed up. She couldn't remember ever playing in high heels before. Wally ordered a Long Island ice tea for Erica.

"This is alcoholic? It tastes just like regular ice tea," she remarked.

Her balance was getting more off-kilter, and it was taking more energy for her to spit out her thoughts. When she did speak, she could tell she was slurring her words a little. However, she kept beating Wally at pool.

Although feeling somewhat scared, Erica got in the truck to drive the mile back to Wally's place. This was no shabby bachelor pad. It was a top-notch apartment with plush white carpet and couches, bright red throw pillows, and black marble countertops on the bar. He also had a to-die-for home theater.

Wally asked Erica if she liked jazz. She said she did, but she didn't know any song titles or jazz singers, so Wally introduced her to some of his favorite tunes while he mixed a drink he thought she would like: a Cosmopolitan. The atmosphere was gentle and seducing.

As the two sat together and relaxed, Wally leaned over and opened a drawer next to the couch. He pulled out a beautifully wrapped gift. Erica read the words on the card:

To my new joy, Erica.
It is my prayer that as we grow closer to
each other, we grow closer to our God.
I want His love to grow in us,
Wally

What was he doing? She had a boyfriend. She couldn't be receiving gifts and notes from someone else. She didn't know what to do, but her curiosity beat out her sense of decency, as she so wanted to open the gift.

"I made this for you, Erica. I hope this will be a special year for us."

He was a gem. He was romantic, charming, and full of surprises, and he knew how to make her feel like a million dollars.

"I also believe God has a special plan for you and me."

What could she say? Life was getting both more

enjoyable and more difficult at the same time. She carefully unwrapped the gift, fighting guilt with each move. She pulled the box away from the wrapping paper and lifted the lid.

Wally had made a necklace for her that had a tiny triangle made of pewter. On the top was a cross, and on the lower corners was the symbol for a boy and a girl. It was to represent the idea that when people grow closer to God, it also brings their relationship closer to each other, creating a special bond that nonbelievers can't experience.

Now her words were haunting her. She had seemingly replaced the cross with another symbol for a boy, and the whole triangle thing was askew.

Whenever Erica could push her guilty conscience aside, she managed to quite enjoy the evening. However, the gift Wally had made her kept eating away at her conscience. She certainly wasn't feeling closer to God. It was nearly two o'clock, and she was feeling the pressure to get home. She tried to get the conversation to a natural place to mention her desire to leave, but then Wally said something that made Erica curious. He mentioned the first time he saw her, but she knew he wasn't referring to their first date.

"Had you seen me before our first date?" The question had to be asked.

"Yes," he admitted.

"So you already knew what I looked like before our date. Where did you see me?"

"Where there is a will, I have my ways." He said it very teasingly.

"Do you actually do business with Margie's company or not?" Erica wanted answers.

"Are you going to pull the truth from me or allow me to keep my dignity?"

She wondered what he had meant. "Three guesses, first two don't count."

Erica's spirit was starting to liven up again. She wanted to know what secret he had to disclose, but her playful sarcasm didn't seem to have a positive effect on Wally.

Wally finally broke the silence. "Do you remember talking with an Officer Devers?"

"Yeah—what's that got to do with it?"

"He asked a lot of questions about your roommate, right?"

"Yeah."

"Well, he was actually checking her out for me. Back then, I only knew Margie by her voice over the phone. But as you well know, I found out that she was a Christian, so I wanted to see if she was cute or not. I needed a way to meet her, but instead of meeting her that night, I met you. Then I had to go to a Plan B to get a date with you."

"But that policeman wasn't you—I would have remembered *you*."

"No, but I was his silent partner, Officer Collins. I just kept staring down at my pad, taking notes the whole time, but I saw enough of you to know what I want—"

"Wait a minute, so the whole, 'I just want to learn how to date a Christian' stuff was just a ploy?"

Wally was trying to keep from being completely rattled. "Don't interrupt. You see, I had my day job, which involved talking to Margie, but I would moonlight at night."

"You're a cop? Oh, my goodness, I can't believe ..."

"No, I'm not a cop."

"Then what? You're not a thief, are you? Did you steal the uniforms and badges? Wait, I saw the names Collins and—and the other guy's—"

"Devers. They were just props."

"So you're an actor. A real actor?"

"In a sense, yes."

"Keep going. We don't have all night."

She was growing impatient with curiosity but delighting in the suspense; she was loving this version of twenty questions that was playing out, especially since it enabled her to squelch her guilt some more.

He hesitated and then finally mumbled, "I used to moonlight as an exotic dancer." Her jaw dropped. "Of course, I had quit the job prior to that night, but I still had easy access to my old uniform, and I convinced my pal "Devers" to help me. He was still working the club."

"Okay, shock me. You had better not be pulling my leg." His look told her it was all true, but Erica still couldn't grasp the idea that an ex-stripper was now wooing her.

Once again, she was reminded of her naïveté. She was starting to question if she had even grown up in this world at all, or whether she had just recently been transported into another world, far removed from the Christian world of her upbringing. This new world was filled with new enticements and experiences at every turn. She couldn't take all these things hitting her at once. She sat still. It took a while for her to settle her mind; when she finally did, she asked Wally to take her home.

"Erica, I understand you wanting to go home, but I've had too much to drink. Better you just stay here tonight."

The next thing Erica knew, she was sobbing. She had vowed she would never sleep with a guy, and she certainly didn't want to leave any suspicion in anyone's mind that she had. She knew she had made some terrible mistakes, and now all she wanted to do was be safe in bed, her bed.

"I can't stay. It won't look right, and it doesn't feel right."

"But I'm thinking of your best interest—and mine.

With all the drunks out tonight on the streets, and me added to the mix, it's not safe. I'm just being practical; plus, I could get a DUI. The cops probably have checkpoints all over the city."

Erica decided to spend the rest of the night at his place, but she also made a decision to clear up the relationship that was developing between them. She didn't want to continue this downward spiral. It seemed like when she tried to live right, she easily talked herself into making bad choices. She thought it was too hard to live a holy life— just too hard. She mustered up some strength to end her relationship with Wally before the night was over.

"Wally, I've failed you. I actually have a boyfriend. I'm a selfish person; I should have shown you what a quality Christian relationship would look like, not the weak, mess-of-a-girl I presented to you. Please know, not all Christian girls are like me. Some really do show their love for God in their actions. I didn't really do that. I was too taken by you, and I need to ask you to forgive me for being so selfish. I think I learned more about your secular lifestyle than you did about my Christian one."

Wally finally offered the following comment: "I guess I did have some wrong ideas about this whole Christian dating stuff, and you did help me. But you're also sort of like my lump of kryptonite. I'm still not sure how this all ended up where it did, but I agree: I need to get away from you before we do something we'll both regret. We're apparently not good for each other, at least not right now."

Wally certainly hadn't offered words of comfort, and the evening did not go as hoped. His comments cut to the core of Erica's heart. He didn't make her feel any better, but he had spoken the truth, and that was what she needed to hear.

Erica finally did something right in ending things

with Wally, but the disconcerting part was that she had made so many poor choices in her four dates with him, she didn't know when she'd ever trust herself to make good choices in the future.

chapter twenty-seven

Mitch gave side glances toward Erica as she sat beside Elmer. Although Mitch was glad Elmer had finally come to church, he still wasn't accustomed to seeing a guy sit next to his gal. After months of invitations, Elmer had finally said he'd give church a try. Mitch hoped it was a New Year's resolution, but he was tempted to believe the draw was, perhaps, an interest in Erica herself.

Mitch tried hard to concentrate on the task at hand—teaching his class. The book of Daniel just couldn't be covered in twelve weeks, so his class had continued into the New Year. Upon seeing Elmer sitting there, Mitch rethought his presentation, mentally working ahead through his notes to see if he could naturally work in a gospel presentation.

"So, let's review. In Daniel 10:5–9, who did we say was the man dressed in linen?"

An elderly man raised his hand, and Mitch nodded, indicating approval to respond. Meanwhile, Mitch noticed Erica looking restless and whispering something to Elmer. She stood up and left the class. Mitch was almost relieved, thinking he could concentrate better on teaching his lesson now that she was gone. It was hard for him to admit

Dressed in Fine Linen

his humanness, but he was getting better at not being so possessive; it still took effort.

Mitch knew Erica was a gift from God for sure, but he wanted to guard against her becoming an idol in his life. When he started seminary, he thought about God almost all the time. Now his thoughts usually drifted to daydreaming about Erica. He enjoyed the diversion. He even looked forward to times he could just veg out and remember her smile, her laugh, her frequent touch.

Mitch barely noticed the gap of silence, but a few coughs got him back in the moment. Trying to appear like he hadn't wandered off in thought, he said, "Thank you for that great review. So, let's move on to verses 10–13."

He soon felt the power of the Holy Spirit as he seized an open opportunity to present the gospel. Elmer seemed to be engaged, but Mitch couldn't tell for sure. He finished his remarks and led a benedictory prayer, extending his arms over the class. He felt he had been used to further the kingdom in some way; he felt empowered; he felt great.

As soon as people started to get up from their seats, Mitch headed for Elmer, as if he and Erica were competing for a prize.

Erica caught up with him first and excitedly blurted out, "What did you think? Isn't Mitch the best speaker? I love his class; I'm learning so much. So tell me, what did you think? I want to know."

"It was okay."

"Okay? Just okay? You must have more to say than just 'okay.'"

"Not really. Not now."

"I didn't mean … I'm sorry. Elmer, I'm just excited to have you here, that's all. I'm so sorry."

"I feel really dumb right now," Elmer added quietly.

Erica calmed herself down, demonstrating she could

95

bounce back from having just done more damage than good. "Hey, this lesson … it's not easy to come into a class midstream. And it's all about prophecy and stuff—really hard stuff. I can understand why you'd feel that way." Elmer seemed to be listening. "Mitch encourages our class to read the chapter we're studying ahead of time. I usually get nothing out of it when I just read it by myself. But then Sunday comes, and he starts taking us to different places in the Bible that relate to the passage, and then when he explains it, I start getting excited because I'm finally getting it. When I try to understand it on my own, I just feel drained and worn out, but most of the Bible isn't like that. The rest of it affects my heart more than my brain."

Mitch could see that Elmer had no clue what Erica was saying; he had tuned her out long before she quit talking. Mitch was also picking up that Elmer was anxious to talk with him.

"Mitch, there was one part of your talk—it reminded me of a time I went to a club with my friend Timmy, just after my sixth birthday. We made crafts and had little skits about some super heroes. We even got to go swimming on the last day. I remember hearing that stuff you said."

"Have you gone to church before?"

"Only for a funeral and my cousin Jim's wedding. This is my first time in a church for no reason."

"Well, the worship service is starting; come sit with Erica and me. Our senior pastor, Pastor Gray, will be preaching."

After the service, Elmer was leaning on the wall, waiting to leave. After all, he really only knew Erica; he hardly knew Mitch, and he vaguely remembered Gabriella. He wanted to bolt from there, but then Gabriella invited him to eat out with the singles. Although he said he appreciated the offer, he declined it. Mitch offered to give him a ride back home while Erica followed them in her car. Mitch had mixed emotions. He wanted to see Elmer grow in faith, but he also wanted Erica all to himself.

As Mitch buckled in, he said, "So, Elmer, tell me. What was the best thing you noticed today?"

Elmer thought for a while and then replied, "I thought it was cool that your pastor works out."

"Oh. Yeah, I guess he does."

"It's important. Have you noticed how most religious guys look like wimps? A real turnoff."

"You obviously work out. Where do you go?"

"I just lift at the apartment. I can't afford anything fancy."

"Can I join you some time? I don't know if our schedules will ever cross, but if I'm going to be a pastor, I guess I'd better start working out."

"Sure. I'm okay with that."

"Will I see you at church next week?"

Elmer got fidgety. "It was okay, but I prefer sleeping in my bed to sleeping in a church."

Erica parked her car and went in to change her clothes while the two guys continued their conversation. She was soon ready to join Mitch and the gang for lunch. Elmer offered his seat to Erica and then closed the passenger door and sent them on their way.

chapter twenty-eight

Today was the second time Mitch had seen Jared (his academic rival) having lunch with Professor Wood after morning classes. Mitch wanted to be the one sitting under the tutelage of Professor Wood; he wanted to be the one noticed as the next great preacher, like Tony Evans or Chuck Swindoll. In his heart, Mitch hoped Jared and Wood were just discussing the troubles of raising teens. Reality was, everyone wanted an audience with Wood, but Jared was the only one who seemed to have one.

Mitch knew his heart was straying from where it should be, so right there, in the cafeteria's corner, he opened his Bible and spent some time in prayer, allowing the scriptures to speak to him. God spoke, prompting him to confess his petty jealousy. God also reminded him about Elmer. Mitch was reminded of his talk with Elmer about working out and felt led to prioritize spending time building his body and building his friendship with Elmer.

Mitch talked to God about his concern that he wouldn't find much in common with Elmer, leaving it in God's hands to enable him to fulfill this calling.

chapter twenty-nine

Tuesday and Saturday mornings seemed to be the only days Elmer and Mitch could work out together. It wasn't ideal for bodybuilding, but Mitch appreciated being able to learn from Elmer, who had been training since his freshman year in high school and knew the art of lifting. Mitch was humbled as he struggled to do even simple things, but he was already feeling the improvement.

That Tuesday, Elmer came up with another one of his unique questions. In Mitch's mind, Elmer asked some really random questions, but he felt obligated to answer them, although coming up with appropriate answers was often a stretch. It was a different kind of stretching than the cerebral questions of seminary. Elmer's questions always touched a different part of Mitch. Maybe it was his heart, maybe it was just that other side of his brain, but he liked Elmer's questions.

"So, what do I suppose dogs think of God, eh? That's today's question? Well, the way I see it, the only example of God that dogs will ever see is what they see in their master. If their master feeds them and plays with them and seeks to train them, I guess they'd see God as a good God. However, if their master beats them or neglects them,

I guess they would have a negative image of God. After all, dogs can't read the Bible to find out the truth about God like we can."

Elmer told Mitch he liked the way he didn't just dismiss his questions like so many others had in the past; Mitch made him feel respected. In his own way, Elmer continued to challenge Mitch through his unique slant on life. He was simple in nature, but ironically, he brought up some really profound concepts.

chapter thirty

Gabriella had invited Erica and Mitch over to eat lunch with her and Johannes.

"Come in, come in." Gabriella had on a cute appliqué apron and was playing hostess.

"My, what a beautiful place you have." Erica couldn't believe that Gabriella, who drove around in a beat-up old Honda, lived in such a posh apartment.

"The company set me up here for my first six months. I have another two months, and then I need to decide if I want to sign for a longer lease."

"Do you think you'll actually move from here?"

"This place is a bit much for me, but when I looked at smaller places, I found they were actually more expensive. So I don't know. They give the company an incredible deal."

Erica knew Gabriella cared about the poor in the world and wanted to live a simple lifestyle. Funny thing was, every time she tried to simplify, God would just bless her and make it hard for her to do it. Gabriella had a great job, but Erica figured she gave much of her income to missions and extra to church, too. Although she rarely read books, she did find Gabriella's suggestion of *Rich Christians in an*

Age of Hunger to be quite challenging. At first, she thought Gabriella's lifestyle would cramp her own, but she never, ever made her feel judged. Gabriella had a calling on her life and shared it with those who were curious, but she never imposed it on others. Erica really admired that in her.

Erica continued the conversation, saying, "Well, you just enjoy this place then, and we will, too. That pool outside looks delightful. Speaking of delightful, where are those guys of ours?"

"I think they went to the three-season room. Johannes has been doing some painting out there; he says the lighting is perfect. We can join them."

The ladies met up with the guys, admired the paintings, and then they all ate a light meal of crepes with yogurt, fruit, chocolate, and granola toppings—carb city.

Erica finally got to put her toes in the gorgeous glass-enclosed pool she'd been admiring. The early spring weather was splendid, and she was with her three favorite friends. It promised to be a wonderful afternoon, but she quickly chilled and went inside to warm up.

On the way home, Erica wasn't her usual self. Mitch even sensed she was perhaps frustrated. He asked her what was wrong; he could see she was being uncharacteristically quiet. She didn't respond. She wouldn't talk about it, and Mitch didn't know what to do, so he just kept driving till they got to Erica's apartment.

Once they arrived, however, he wanted answers. "You can't keep this to yourself. Tell me, what's going on in that pretty head of yours?"

Mitch waited. There was silence. He finally gave up

and reached for the radio when she said, "Answer this question: What did you think about the way Gabriella and Johannes interacted at the pool?"

"I wasn't really paying attention. Was there a problem?"

"Ugh! No, there was no problem."

"Then why are you so upset?"

Silence enveloped the car, almost suffocating Erica.

"Are you blind? He was so attentive to her. He whispered in her ear what I'd guess were kind, sweet, romantic words. He touched her—often. They even ..." She couldn't bring herself to say the word *kissed*.

"Kissed? Yeah, they're like that, I've noticed. Are you upset because our relationship isn't like that?"

"No comment."

"Do you want it to be?"

"Do I have to spell it out? Mitch, you've never even put your arm around me or hugged me romantically in all the time we've been dating. Why not? How could you not?"

With that, Mitch put his arm behind Erica. It felt as comforting as a two-by-four. She pushed it away. Now he was really confused.

"Mitch, other guys desire to kiss me. I know. I've kissed guys since we've met." She had Mitch's undivided attention now. "And a big question in my mind has been why have *they* yearned to kiss me, but you haven't? Why have they made that move and you haven't? I figured it was your dedication to purity, but you are a man, aren't you? Don't you have any desire for me? Any at all?"

Mitch was silent. She had put herself on the line and was obviously waiting for some response. He finally asked if he could hold her hand and pray with her.

"Are you kidding?"

She got out of the car and slammed the door as hard as she could. She didn't even say goodbye. Mitch watched her as she ran up the steps. She struggled to find her keys and get the door open.

Mitch sat in the car, taking in what had just happened. He couldn't believe she admitted to kissing other guys. Who were these guys? Had she kissed Elmer? No, he was too ... or was he? Mitch had to know. He opened the car door and walked over to Elmer's place. *Knock, knock.* No answer. Maybe he's sleeping. Mitch pounded on Elmer's door till his knuckles stung. Still no answer. He decided to check the weight room. Success. Elmer was working out.

"Hey, how's it going, Buddy? You almost done?" Mitch felt dishonest sounding so cheerful, but he didn't want to betray his purpose.

"Hi, Mitch." A few grunts later, "Yeah, just two more sets. You come to work out?"

"Nah, just thought we could talk."

"Sure, man." Mitch now had his opportunity, but how was he going to bring this up? He didn't want to believe Elmer had kissed his woman, and he didn't want to reveal his true feelings; not to Elmer, anyway.

Elmer grabbed his towel and flung it over his shoulders. "Jus' need to cool down. Give me a minute to jump in the pool."

Mitch decided to just go for it. After all, they had spent many days working out together and building a relationship. "Elmer, you have a girlfriend?"

"No one steady. Why?"

"Ah, I was, ah, thinking maybe we could double-date if you did." It was a quick recovery.

"I don't think my girls would mix well with you and Erica."

"Why not? You don't date women like Erica, do you?" He seized his opportunity.

"Oh, Erica is fine, don't get me wrong, but girls like her don't quite meet my needs."

"Oh." Mitch was not sure he should pursue this, but he had to know. "So you've never been romantic with Erica, I take it."

Elmer seemed on edge. "What do you mean? Did she say something?"

Mitch interpreted Elmer's response as a statement of guilt. To be sure, he decided to dig further. "Well, you two are friends, but did you ever pursue more with her, like a kiss or anything?"

"A gentleman would never tell."

Mitch figured Elmer used that line often. But, in effect, Mitch knew Elmer had indeed kissed his woman. He dropped the conversation and turned it to lighter subject matter, but his body felt the weight of what was left unspoken.

As Mitch walked to his car, he peered toward Erica's apartment, wondering if he should let her know he was still there. He drove a quarter-mile down the street and then did a U-turn and came back to Erica's place. He sat a minute and then went up her stairs. He couldn't handle leaving things the way they were.

Knock, knock. "Erica, please, open up. It's me, Mitch. Please?"

"It's open."

He entered the room. Pachabel's "Cannon" was playing softly. Erica was sitting in the bend of the couch, looking all red-faced and puffy. She looked so sad; it melted his heart, causing an incredible ache. He moved slowly to sit near her. They sat in silence, just listening to each other breathe. There were no words to speak. Mitch's mind was busy processing what had taken place earlier. He had no direction, no opinion, and no plan. He didn't know how to fix this one. His emotions were like an alternating current; he felt guilty for a time, then foolish, then he'd jump back into acts of mental rage. He thought Erica could have been kinder, under the circumstances.

chapter thirty-one

Erica wasn't sure this would work, but she figured she'd give it a try. As awkward as it seemed, she knew her evening with Mitch would end in a kiss. He had promised it. She wanted spontaneity, but she had waited long enough in vain. Could she even enjoy it? But after almost three weeks without alone time with Mitch, she was hoping for a new beginning.

The evening started out beautifully. Mitch had brought over ingredients to make a beef stir-fry in oyster sauce. He was doing his chef magic in her kitchen. She stepped out to get some fortune cookies and chopsticks; the meal had needed a few touches of authenticity.

Their Chinese Valentine dinner had been a success; the sun was going down, and the moment had come. It was indeed awkward, but Mitch leaned in for a kiss, as promised. It was obvious that he was not comfortable at all; his body was shaking, and the look in his eyes said it all before his lips expressed a thing. "I just can't. It reminds me too much of—"

Erica was devastated, but not because of Mitch's

actions. She was devastated at who she had become. She felt so selfish. Months earlier, Mitch shared with her how he had been violated as a child. He had never talked about it with anyone before her, and now he was coming face-to-face with this ghost haunting him. Erica had seen a photo of his perpetrator. Erica had silently noted how much they looked alike. Again, they seemed to be at a loss for what to do, how to fix this.

"Erica, I'm so sorry."

"It's okay. I understand."

"Maybe it's just not God's plan for me to be married."

"Nonsense. You obviously thought it was fine all year. You believed in us, didn't you? In a future? We talked about marriage, about a future. This is just the beginning; don't give—"

"You deserve something, something I can't promise. I always believed that if God provided a wife for me, He'd provide the passion and ability to express my love to her. Maybe I was wrong. I always said I wouldn't be like my dad, but I'm turning into him. I need to save you from that nightmare."

"I don't know where you are going with this, but I don't like it. Back up to what you said about God. You see, that's what I love about you. You trust God with everything, even this. You trust God to provide you with passion. That's what I admire about you, Mitch. It's so neat to spend time with a guy who actually relies on God, who isn't just a macho narcissist. Mitch, we can do this."

"You have the heart of an angel, but Erica, I know you kissed Elmer. You said yourself that there were guys. Doesn't that tell you something about your need? Your desire? Your passion?"

"But ..."

She wished she could say it meant nothing, but

she knew it'd be a lie. She had indeed enjoyed those encounters with other guys. She felt shame seize her, and just as suddenly, depression fell over her like a thick blanket. Condemnation was finding a way into her soul and beating her down. She wanted to die.

chapter thirty-two

The following Sunday, Erica decided to visit a popular local church. She didn't feel like seeing Mitch right after their last encounter, and she knew he had to go to church and teach his lesson. For his sake, she hoped he wouldn't be flooded with questions about why she wasn't there.

The ladies at the new church asked her to attend their class. She found them all so friendly and inviting. They were doing a study on Daniel, as well. She thought it a bit coincidental, but she knew God had spoken to her through Daniel's life, and she figured there was more for her to learn.

The class had already met to discuss their homework, and now they were settling in to watch a video. Daniel 5 was on the agenda. The focus turned to the vessels that had been brought from Jerusalem to Babylon. The gold vessels from the temple that had been stored were now being taken out to be used at a party in an unholy way—vessels that had been pronounced holy by God in the past. Next, referencing 2 Timothy and Ezra, the teacher explained that these very vessels that had been treated as unholy could be treated as holy again. The message was brought home to the ladies as the speaker related how so many women struggle because they have used their vessels for unholy purposes, but that God desires to redeem them and use them for holy purposes again. Toward the end of the DVD, the ladies were asked to stand and proclaim words of consecration, stating publicly the truth from God's Word. Erica joined in, repeating the phrases after the speaker:

I belong to Jesus. *I belong to Jesus.*

I am a holy vessel because ... *I am a holy vessel because ...*

The Holy Spirit of the Living God lives in me. *The Holy Spirit of the Living God lives in me.*

The Lord has said over me, *The Lord has said over me,* "I declare you holy." *"I declare you holy."*

The tears began as she said that line.

Today I resolve to trust what He says. *Today I resolve to trust what He says.*

I am holy. *I am ho—*

Now the words were hard to choke out as she felt their truth, yet they gave her inner strength. It seemed she was only able to say a few words before she was choked up again, but she persisted.

Enable me daily, Spirit of God,
to recognize myself as holy.
Open my eyes to every ploy of Satan
that lies to me and says I am not.
You, God, are the True God.
Your Word is truth.
This day, Father, I choose to trust You.
In Jesus's name, Amen.

Tears streamed down Erica's face. Sobs could be heard amongst the crowd, but she only thought of her own. She couldn't hide them. The words had taken effort to speak out, but she had managed to get most of them out and actually believe them.

She felt a warm power invade her body as she spoke the words—words of deliverance. Soon after, she felt a washing effect pour over her, and she felt free. Erica had hope. She again felt she could make good decisions for the future. She desired to be a woman God would someday be proud to call His bride—a woman who would be "dressed in fine linen, bright and clear." She loved that passage from Revelation 19 and how it made her feel cherished and valued. She wanted to be that bride.

Erica had heard people say, "God has made you holy, now act it." It usually came across as a judgment, a burden. Now she wanted to do just that. Now she understood that acting holy wasn't a game of pretend but an aligning of her actions to match who she had been declared to be, with who she really was. She was that women "dressed in fine linen, bright and clear," and she'd never let herself forget that. She knew her true Bridegroom.

chapter thirty-three

It struck Erica as strange. How could she have been on such a spiritual high just a week ago, and now she was struggling with depression again? She decided to take a stroll in the evening air to relax and found herself walking along the highway, cars whizzing by, and she wondered how she'd even gotten there. Just then, a car mirror brushed her as she carelessly stepped onto the highway. It jolted her back to reality.

Her nerves were shot. It scared her to think she didn't even remember walking up to the highway. She anxiously found her way back to her street and returned to her door. As she entered the apartment, she saw an additional body. It seemed Margie had found herself a boyfriend. Snuggled together under a blanket, it appeared the two of them had fallen asleep watching a movie.

Erica quietly made her way to the bedroom, but she yelped when she stubbed her toe upon entering the bathroom. When she came out, they were both gone, but she was glad. She needed to be alone—alone with God.

Life had a way of whizzing around her, and right now, she wanted calmness. She wanted to be able to pray out loud. She was finally ready to confess—both who her God was, and who she had been.

"God, You protected me and kept me safe even when I chose a bad way. You love me, even when I do things that could cause myself harm. It's just that sometimes I hate who I am, and I feel I deserve harm. I feel totally unworthy of forgiveness. I know I am forgiven, but I keep remembering the people I've hurt. Unfortunately, my being forgiven doesn't automatically fix their lives. Yet, I guess in some ways I'm glad I've fallen so far. It's allowed me to know how wonderful it really is to feel loved and forgiven, and it'll keep me from being so judgmental of others who have had more difficult lives and have fallen even further into sin. I see just how great Your salvation really is to mankind. I like how Johannes puts it, that Your gift of salvation and forgiveness feels like someone just paid your thirty-year mortgage. I second that feeling.

"I guess since I grew up in a Christian home, it was hard to really appreciate what it meant to be forgiven since my sins always seemed so insignificant compared to others. I guess it wasn't until I saw how strong my will could be, and how much of a fight I could put up, and that I'd choose to defraud my brothers through selfish games instead of choose You, that I realized what a depraved individual I really am. Now I truly value the joy and peace and love You give. It is priceless.

"I want to share this with the world, so they can know such freedom. The way won't always be easy, and I'll still battle with my will from time to time, but I never want to repeat these past months again. It's hard to live with a sinner, and when the sinner is yourself, there's no escape but through repentance. I yearn for Your shalom. I need that kind of peace, that kind of wholeness. Good night, God. I so love You! In Jesus's name, Amen."

chapter thirty-four

Gabriella and Johannes came by the apartment to show off her engagement ring. It had been Johannes's grandmother's ring, ornate and beautiful. It was easy to be happy for them since they obviously were a match. Erica felt a twinge of jealousy, but more than that, she questioned her own readiness to get married. Mitch still captured her interest, filling a niche in her life, a spiritual connection of sorts. Still, she knew they weren't ready for marriage. Erica wondered how some couples could be ready to commit themselves for life after just three months of dating, and others were still working at it nine months later, sometimes years later.

Gabriella spoke for them both: "We set the date for April 7, and we're hoping you two can help us with our special day."

"Sure, what can we do?"

"Erica, I want you to play *The Lord's Prayer* on your violin. Would you?"

"I hardly ever play anymore, but for you, I'll pull it out of the closet. I'd be honored. And I'm so happy for you both."

Johannes crossed the room, put his arm around Mitch,

and added, "We'd like to have a small tent reception on the church lawn, and we are hoping you'll be our emcee."

"Double honored. I'd love to."

"Great. I think we'll have around seventy people at the reception—just family and a few close friends. We want to make it a day of getting to know each other's family and friends better. We can talk details over some ribs and beans later on. How does that sound?"

"Great. But it seems like we should go celebrate now. Any suggestions?" Mitch looked around, fishing for a response.

Johannes took the lead. "We were planning to do a few more errands, but Gabriella, what do you say we go out and celebrate with these guys?"

Gabriella nodded approval. "How about dessert at Olive Garden? They have the best coffee there, too."

Erica couldn't fall asleep. It could have been the coffee doing its thing, but she didn't get to sleep the night before, either. She kept thinking about the missionary moment at church earlier in the week. Was she being called to be a missionary? She'd never really considered it before. But there was a fleeting moment back in high school that kept haunting her. She would have dismissed it, but she wondered why it was so easily retrieved from her memory. She could still picture walking up to the visiting missionary, waiting for his attention, and saying, "I feel called to missions." Oh, and when she clarified that she was a freshman in high school and not a freshman in college, she knew the speaker simply didn't believe what she was saying was worth a hoot. Is that why she remembered it, because she'd felt offended? Or was it something God wanted her to remember for some other reason?

She took some kava kava, hoping it'd calm down her overactive mind, and decided to see if there was anyone available to chat on-line.

The list of people who were on-line included the usual: Cassie, Felly, Fufe, Jennifer, Justin, Lil, Mari, of course Mitch, Nikki, Sherilyn, and Travis (the old high school youth leader from Bethel). Erica decided to chat with him for a change.

EEW: John 10:10
Travis, you there?

Wndx_kps_me_frm_streakin:
Maybe

EEW: John 10:10
Funny. You're never on this time of night

Wndx_kps_me_frm_streakin:
Remember, our family just moved to Indonesia so it's only the afternoon here.

EEW: John 10:10
Well, I can't sleep.

Wndx_kps_me_frm_streakin:
Why not?

EEW: John 10:10
Overactive mind

Wndx_kps_me_frm_streakin:
Something bothering you?

EEW: John 10:10
No. Well, maybe. I was thinking about being a missionary—and don't laugh, I could be serious.

Wndx_kps_me_frm_streakin:
What got that on your mind?

EEW: John 10:10
Well, really it's the boyfriend issue. You know Mitch and I have been dating for like nine months. Is that long enough to know if we should get married?

Wndx_kps_me_frm_streakin:
It's long enough to make a baby, but I don't think time is an indicator for marriage. There are just too many factors to consider. Do you feel ready for that type of life commitment?

EEW: John 10:10
I guess I'd like to get married, and I guess I'm ready to do it. I know Mitch brought it up months ago, but if he were to ask me today, I'm still not sure how I'd answer him. I think I'd say yes.

Wndx_kps_me_frm_streakin:
So, all he needs to do is ask?

EEW: John 10:10

It's not that simple. See, I want to say yes because he's a wonderful guy. I'm just not sure we're meant for each other. How can I know he's the one?

Wndx_kps_me_frm_streakin:

The age-old question with the age-old answer—you'll just know. But I suggest you ask God for a sign. Either ask for a sign to know you should break up, or ask for one to know you should get married.

EEW: John 10:10

I'll do that. I'll pray that something BIG gets in the way of us getting married if we shouldn't do it. The Lord knows how much I want him. Sound fair?

Wndx_kps_me_frm_streakin:

Sorry, but I have to take my little Lessee to her lesson. Be sure and keep me posted on what happens. I sure miss all you "kids"—ha. The past five years have flown! Now you are all done with college, on your own, and seriously talking marriage. It makes me feel old. Nancee and I are going to be celebrating our tenth anniversary in a few days. I just saw your question—yeah, sounds fair. I'll be praying for you as well. Keep the faith.

EEW: John 10:10

Thx. Bye.

Erica looked at the clock. 2:14 a.m. She hoped to get some sleep.

chapter thirty-five

Erica joined Mitch and his parents after playing her violin. She vowed to never play at a friend's wedding again, as she had to concentrate on the notes and couldn't watch the bridesmaids walk down the aisle. However, she and Mitch finally got to attend a wedding together, and now she could relax and drink it all in. Having his parents visiting was just an added blessing. Gabriella looked so pure, and her face was so radiant. Her auburn hair was done up and looked so elegant. Erica had been looking forward to hearing them recite their vows. She wanted to know what two people really promise to each other on their wedding day. Young, naïve, in-love couples all over the world make promises before God and their loved ones, but many of those same people later break those vows. Maybe they just forget what they ever said to each other, what they vowed before God. Erica promised herself that if she married, she'd frame their vows and keep them somewhere they could easily remind themselves of their promises. Erica so wanted Gabriella and Johannes to be able to keep the vows they were about to make to each other. She listened to every promise.

"Gabriella, today I take you to be my wife. I am confident that it was God's will that brought us together. I will provide for your needs as Christ provides our every need. My desire is to be the initiator in keeping God's will in every area of our lives. I promise to provide the right atmosphere for you so that you may grow into all that God intended for you to be. Being one in our Lord's sight will encourage me to share my whole self with you. As we turn to the future, whether it means prosperous or difficult times, my prayer is that God will be glorified through our lives together."

"Johannes, today I take you to be my husband. I am confident that God has brought us together. I promise to love, honor, and cherish you. I promise to love you consistently and to be a source of encouragement and support for you. I will trust you to provide for our needs as Christ provides our every need. My earnest prayer is that I will share openly my thoughts and feelings, that we may be truly one as God intended, and as one, keep God's will for our lives together."

Erica basked in the hope of Mitch proclaiming his love and devotion to her in front of their families someday. She noticed Mitch giving her hand an extra squeeze just then and tried to imagine whether she could promise those same things. She noticed the absence of the phrase, "till death do us part." Did they not promise that for a reason, or did they just not like the idea of reciting such a morbid thought on their wedding day? And don't they have to include the "in sickness and in health" part, as well?

Mitch was busy once the reception started. He constantly had to leave the dinner table to go to the microphone. He was doing a rather keen job of keeping the atmosphere fun and lively. Erica hadn't seen his vibrant side before; she felt proud of him, and it was making her fall in love with him even more. He was really learning to loosen up, and she could see that he had a lot to offer the world. He could be quite the comedian—a side she hadn't seen except one-on-one with her. She was enjoying the process of seeing this man unfold before her very eyes.

chapter thirty-six

Personal letters were a rarity, so when Erica received one, she had a ritual she would follow. She would get cleaned up and put on her jammies, mix up a cup of Carnation hot cocoa and sit in her favorite cozy, forest-green chair. She would then use her favorite Norwegian pewter letter opener to slit open the envelope.

Mitch's opened letter was now in her hand, and she expectantly lifted the folds. The ritual was much longer than the note, but not wasted. In fact, he wrote very little.

It simply said, "Sweetie, I love you. Mitch."

She stared at the words, pressed the letter to her chest, and closed her eyes. It was all she needed.

Mitch would be coming over to lift weights with Elmer in the morning, and then she and Mitch would have their usual prayer time. Now she hoped to hear an "I love you" face-to-face.

chapter thirty-seven

Mitch came by before working out with Elmer to drop off his stuff, as usual. "Pastor Gray handed me this envelope to give to you. What's it for?"

Erica looked puzzled at first, but then she figured it out. "Oh, that's right. I signed up for more information on that Sunday when the missionary came by. I had forgotten about it until now." She stuck it on the bookshelf.

"Elmer's probably waiting for me. See you in an hour or so. I have to tell you something."

"I'll be waiting." She gave Mitch a wink and a smile, and he gave her a grin from cheek to cheek.

Mitch was all sweaty, so he showered as Erica finished scrubbing the kitchen floor. When he was all cleaned up, he walked into the kitchen, took the sponge out of Erica's wet hand, placed her hand in his, and simply said, "I love you. Will you marry me?"

Erica, desperately in need of a shower herself, looked at Mitch with unbelief and said, "Did I just—? Did you just—? I think I—. Yes, yes, I want to marry you."

It was an expected response; it was the one she had

planned on giving for months, but it came out totally unrehearsed. She had been surprised and totally caught off-guard, even though it was the one-year anniversary of Erica's arrival in Dallas and the anniversary of the day Erica and Mitch first met. May 12 was surely their special day. So much had happened in the past year, and what the next year would hold, only God knew.

chapter thirty-eight

"Hey there, Gabriella. Yoo-hoo, over here," Erica called.

Gabriella walked over to the booth where Erica was sipping orange juice. "I'm so glad you could meet me for breakfast."

Gabriella pulled out her chair while speaking. "I consider it a treat—both being with you and eating out at IHOP. Married life is wonderful, but it changes so many things I hadn't anticipated. For instance, I love waking up on a Saturday morning with my best friend right there beside me. But it's *so* convenient, I don't make the effort to see my other friends as frequently, and I'm missing them—you in particular."

"It must be wonderful—marriage."

"Well, you'll be finding out firsthand before you know it. How are your wedding plans coming along?"

Erica wasn't ready to field that question quite yet, so she redirected the conversation. "Let's order first. I'm starved."

She always liked to get the ordering out of the way anyway, and she knew just what she wanted—cheese blintzes and a pot of coffee with a side of fresh fruit.

Gabriella's order surprised Erica, as she just ordered rye toast, no butter, a poached egg, and a small orange juice.

"So how is the engagement going? I bet you are busy with wedding plans. How big a wedding will it be?" Gabriella finally got the conversation back to the original topic.

Erica had used those ten minutes to get her response prepared. "Everything is great, but we're not really talking much about plans yet. My mom wrote up a guest list and booked the reception at The Manor in West Orange, and I think the church is booked, but that's all."

"It's a good start," Gabriella encouraged. "My favorite part was planning the reception. I had been gathering ideas since I was young, and I was so glad when I finally had my day to put all that planning to good use."

"Your reception was really fun and unique. So after a lifetime of planning, and all the attention to detail, why not invite more people?"

"I love doing all those special extras, and I wanted to do it for all the people who have meant so much to me all my life. Sure, we could have had lots more people, but in the end, I just wanted those who were really close to us."

"I thought those chocolate-covered bride and groom strawberries were adorable. So far, I think we'll have over two hundred at our wedding. It'll be so different from yours."

"Don't get stressed about all the people and trying to play hostess. Just keep your attention on your wonderful Mitch, and remember it's your day."

"I want to get personal. Did you ever have doubts about marrying Johannes? I mean, you only knew each other a few months."

"Not really. After the second date, I probably knew he

was for me. Sure, we have lots to learn about each other still, and some rough spots have already come, but right away, I sensed a mutual destiny for us and a trust that we will conquer whatever comes our way."

Erica hesitated. She knew she could easily bring it up now, but all she said was, "That's so great."

The food smelled delicious as the waitress neared the table. "The blintzes?"

"Those are mine."

"And these must be yours, Miss. Can I bring you ladies anything else?"

"Some honey, please," said Gabriella.

"Be right back."

The waitress had her hair pulled up in a high ponytail that bounced up and down as she walked away. She was so tiny and so young; it was hard to believe she was old enough to work.

"Can I bring up work stuff?" Gabriella asked.

"Sure. It would be nice to talk about it with someone who understands the situation."

"How are things in your department after Wil's big announcement?"

"I don't want to name names, but I'd say all but two seem to be handling it in stride. It was a big blow, but I think some are still in denial that it's really going to affect them come December bonus time."

"Yeah. Maybe some miracle will change that." Gabriella felt she could offer some hope.

"So, let me know if I have it straight. This is still somewhat new to me. What I understand is that Wil had a customer who wanted to purchase some stock on margin, but somehow he missed a zero and didn't get enough stock bought, and that somehow affects year-end bonuses, right?"

"The easy explanation is, the client knew he made a killing, and when he wanted the stock sold two days later, he was expecting millions and only got thousands. He was furious. He showed us proof of his order, and yes, Wil missed not only one zero, but a set of three zeros. Our company has to make up his loss, one way or another. We're not absolutely sure the insurance company won't cover us at this point, as I bet they'll find a loophole. There's more to it, but I can't go into it."

"How do you sleep at night with all this pressure?"

"I know God put me here to be a witness for Him. I wake up each day and ask Him to show me how Jesus would do my job. It seems to change everything about how I do business. I see corruption, I hear lies, I see people abuse each other to get ahead, and much of it is plain ugly. Then God taps me on the shoulder and shows me something He wants me to see. Sometimes, it's an answer to a financial problem, sometimes, it's a sad face that tugs on my heart, and He asks me to bring encouragement. I sleep well each night knowing God directs my steps. He is the one I think to please each day, not my boss, nor my clients, but Him."

"You never lose sleep, not even over this recent incident?"

"I still slept fine, but I did cry over it—often. Wil was a good friend and made great contributions to this company. When I came here, he was one of the first people I was able to connect to. He feels so sorry about what happened. He hasn't found a job, and it may be impossible to find one in the same field for the money he was making. It will probably mean moving his three little boys and his wife from their familiar surroundings, and he's not looking forward to that."

"My problems seem so small when compared to others'."

"Your problems may seem small, but I don't think we can dismiss problems because they are small. They all need attention."

"Well, maybe not small to me, but probably insignificant to others. They say not to sweat the small stuff."

"What's up? You have something to share. And I disagree with that not sweating the small stuff argument. Small stuff sneaks up on people all the time. So, out with it."

Erica got all choked up and headed toward the ladies' room, leaving Gabriella at the table alone. Erica was going to have another tear session.

Gabriella paid the bill and found Erica in the bathroom, dabbing her eyes. It wasn't a very conducive place for talking, so they left the restaurant and walked to a nearby park.

Once seated, Erica let it all spill out: "I don't understand myself. Ever since I met Mitch, I've only seen a wonderful man—a man I would want to marry. I admire him; I love to be with him. I waited eagerly for his first 'I love you,' for every confirmation of love, and I even waited for his proposal. By the time he proposed, it was a no-brainer to reply yes. But now I feel so foolish. I'm sad all the time, we aren't talking like we used to, and everything is such a mess. I've always wanted to plan my wedding, and now I get a sick feeling in me every time my mother asks me about it. Did you go through this?"

"Everyone is different. Tell me what positive things have happened since the proposal?"

"I'd be lying if I said there was nothing good. Oh, it was fun to tell our parents and friends and see their reactions. It was great hearing Mitch recall our story to his parents. That was my favorite part, I guess. Everyone was so encouraging, except Margie, but that's a whole 'nother story."

"We'll have to get back to Margie later. When did you start having all these negative feelings?"

"When people started getting nosey."

"What do you mean?"

"You know, the whole idea that we haven't kissed yet. People either think we're lying, or they think we don't really love each other. How can I convince them we just want to honor God?"

"It's not your job to convince them, but I'm wondering if you're convinced. If you were, I don't think this would bother you like it does."

Gabriella's words hung over Erica like a storm cloud, heavy and gray. She couldn't reply.

"You know, Johannes and I kissed before we were even engaged; I never felt any particular calling to not kiss him. It's between you two and God. God works differently in each person's life. We have freedom in Christ, and we can't impose our calling on others. I feel called to live a simple lifestyle, but it's not a doctrine I go preaching for everyone to follow. It's the same with you and not kissing."

"Well, actually it's not. It was never anything decided between us—it just hasn't happened."

"Oh. Or should I say 'uh-oh' instead? No wonder you are feeling like you are. Have you talked with him about it?"

"A few times, sort of. We just seem to ignore it now. And I was doing a good job of ignoring it too, until everyone started bringing it up. Then I couldn't anymore, and I had to face the fact that this is getting to be something really huge."

"What has he said? Has he given any reason?"

Erica had to be careful to not betray Mitch's confidence, but she still answered truthfully: "I stopped expecting it to happen, and in some ways, it made it easier. Our relationship continued to grow, and he was becoming more fun each month. We seemed to be growing together as a couple."

Gabriella said nothing, so Erica continued, "I keep trying to understand how I got to this place. How could I have allowed myself to get engaged to someone who I can't comfortably talk to about something as simple as kissing?"

"What are you going to do?"

"I don't know."

chapter thirty-nine

"Hello?"

"Hi. It's Gabriella. Would you like to go on a little road trip with Johannes and me? We are going to look at the linguistic center in Duncanville. I hear they have a nice museum, and your name came to mind."

"When are you going?"

"Can you be here by 10:30? Then we can drive together from here."

"Sure."

Gabriella added, "Would you like to invite Mitch to join us?"

"I'll give him a call."

The ride down to Duncanville was rather mundane, but upon leaving the center, the car was buzzing with enthusiasm. Johannes and Gabriella were already talking about leaving their jobs to go back to school to learn how to translate the Bible. Amazingly, Erica was feeling the same tug, but she didn't want to admit it right then. She needed some time to get used to such an idea and determine whether it was legitimate or not. Mitch was very encouraging to Johannes and Gabriella, but, of course, he wasn't engaged to them.

Erica knew things often come in threes. First, it was the missionary at the church, then Mitch delivered the envelope from Pastor Gray (which had been carefully stored, unopened, on her shelf since she got it), and now this was going to be her third exposure to Bible translation. Perhaps God wanted her to get behind Johannes and Gabriella and support them in prayer, support them financially, or support them by encouraging them to pursue this new direction. Yeah, that was probably it.

Erica had only supported one missionary family so far.  Right after she landed her first job downtown, she wanted to personally support a missionary, and she gave $300 as start-up money to a family who was going to work in Greece, as well as make a monthly financial commitment of $25 to them.

She had continued to e-mail the family each month. They always responded, speaking of their antics, or answering her questions about life in Greece, or sharing prayer requests. Even though the Apostle Paul had evangelized that area two thousand years ago, there was still such need for the gospel to be taught.

However, when the couple sent their first thank-you note, they mentioned that they had used the $300 to take a six-week crash course in Greek. She was mad. She thought the money should have been used to do outreach, not language school. By now she was beginning to see how her response was inappropriate. How could they do outreach if they couldn't speak the language? How could they do even the simple tasks of buying gas and food without some ability in the local language? She hoped she'd be more understanding if she took on supporting Johannes and Gabriella.

chapter forty

The same old bus was still transporting Erica to work each day. Traffic on Central Avenue never got any better, but she had learned how to successfully read on the bus so she wouldn't get motion sickness; she held the book in front of her so she wouldn't have to look downward. She closed her recently purchased book written by Marilyn Laszlo about translation work in Papua New Guinea. Months earlier, Erica had written down what she was looking for in a job while reading *Decision Making and the Will of God*, and now she noted how that list lined up with the job of a Bible translator. A match.

On the ride home from work, Erica sat next to an older gentleman. She learned that he was a lawyer and started asking him about job opportunities, mentioning she had always had a dream of working in law. If she didn't marry a pastor, her second choice was to marry a lawyer or become one. She had always loved the drama of her philosophy classes in college—the mind challenges, the splitting of hairs over minute nuances of meaning, the intellectual arguments, the passion. She could envision dramatic, mind-stimulating dinner conversations when her man came home from work when she'd ask how his day had gone.

The gentleman's words brought her back to the moment. "My recommendation to you would be to further your education if you are serious about a job in law."

"Oh, actually, I've recently been thinking about continuing my education, but I've been looking into the area of linguistics, not law." She surprised herself with her response.

"What will you use that for?"

"I've been thinking about working as a Bible translator in a remote village where people don't have the Bible in their language." Erica couldn't believe what she just told this complete stranger.

"You're ringing my chimes," he said. "We support a couple who does Bible translation. Great people."

Her conversation with this complete stranger—this angel from God—made her again wonder if translation was really something she should be considering. She decided to fill out the application that had been sitting on her bookshelf—no commitment, just gingerly take the next step. It seemed like she was walking on a frozen pond, wondering when the ice would be too thin, and she'd just fall in, but for now, she had decided to take a first, very hesitant, step.

chapter forty-one

Gabriella saw Erica at the mall and ran over to see what all she had bought.

"Gabriella, fancy meeting you here." Erica bent to give her a hug.

"So what did you get, Erica? I see you have two bags. What's in them?"

"Oh, I needed a white blouse and found just what I was looking for in the first store I went to. Then I just perused the shops for a good bargain or two. I found some new PJs 50 percent off and a pair of jeans with a rebate for twenty dollars. You up for a smoothie? I could use a break from being alone."

"I'm in." Gabriella was always ready to chat.

The two of them sat sipping their green tea frappuccinos at a small round table. Two very handsome men had caught Erica's attention, and she found herself trying to overhear their conversation. She could tell they were talking about her and Gabriella. The guys caught Erica looking at them and quickly started up a conversation.

"Excuse me, ladies, you seem to be having a nice time talking, but I was wondering if you could help us out?"

Oh, brother. What a lame come-on line. Erica looked

at Gabriella to see how they should handle this. Gabriella took the lead.

"How can we help you?"

"Could you tell us what makes you happy?"

Erica wondered whether Gabriella would take this chance to witness, or would she throw the question back at them.

"Nothing makes me happy, but I'm very happy."

Erica thought Gabriella's response was clever. The game had begun.

"Miss, what makes you happy?" This time the question was directed to Erica.

Erica was disappointed. She wanted to see the game get played out between Gabriella and the guys and just watch.

"Nothing clever from me. I'm happy when I'm at peace with myself."

"Do you know how to be at peace with yourself?" asked the taller guy.

"Yes, and it's all based on my relationship with Jesus." Erica decided to go for broke. "I'm also planning to dedicate my life to translating the Bible for people in remote villages in Papua New Guinea—my effort to spread peace."

That should take care of any question about where she stood, but she wondered why she played the Bible translation card again. It seemed to just roll off the tip of her tongue so easily.

"Dynamo! You guys are Christians! This is my friend Mac, and I'm James, but call me Jamie. We just started taking courses at the seminary."

"I'm Gabriella, and this is my friend Erica. Nice to meet you."

Mac looked at Erica and asked, "So, you are going to be a Bible translator?"

"Honestly, I was thinking we should try and get rid of you guys since my friend Gabriella is newly married. But to answer your question, yes, the two of us have been thinking about doing it—Gabriella more than me, though."

"Ah, here we meet two fine women, one married and the other maybe going off to faraway lands."

Erica chose not to mention that she had a fiancé—a fiancé who happened to attend the same seminary they did. She suddenly felt self-conscious about her left hand and kept it neatly tucked under the table.

Erica was in the mood to write down another prayer. It was becoming a regular passion of hers these past months.

"Father God, let's forget the formalities. Bottom line, do I even know how to hear Your voice? I'm guessing I probably need to break up with Mitch, don't I? But I'd rather have it work out for us—it would just be easier that way. I don't want to go through all the shame and humiliation of a breakup, all the questions and explanations. Send me to a secluded island, please!

"How could I have let this go on for so long? Why did I? Was I just desperate to get married? Or was I jealous of Gabriella's relationship with Johannes? Or Margie's mystery man? Do I understand anything at all about love? What will Mitch say—will this devastate him? Ruin him? What have I done? I've been so unfair to him. He's such a nice guy, which makes it so easy to enjoy his company and to hang on his every word, but the reality is, we shouldn't be together, right? Am I just being selfish? Or am I finally being wise? Is this just

cold feet? Or is it You answering my prayer to not have peace if we shouldn't continue our relationship?

"And then there's the whole linguistic thing. I can't believe I think I'm being called to be a missionary. What will people say when they hear about my plans? Well, that is, if I really do it. And I'm a bit mad—why call me to go when I'm engaged to a guy who is planning to serve in the States? He's a man dedicated to working for You, even? Maybe he's supposed to change his plans and go overseas, too. Is that Your plan? But he seems so sure You want him here. And how can he know? Maybe You do have new plans for him.

"Is this calling the big thing I prayed about—that if Mitch and I shouldn't get married, You'd put a big thing in the way? Or is the big thing the lack of romance? Or our lack of communicating? Well, how many big things do I need before I start living in light of what You've shown me, huh?

"And I can't believe all the times the translation thing keeps coming up. God, are You crazy? I hope that's not inappropriate, but there are so many better people to put on the mission field—why me? I'm definitely lacking in many departments. I always heard that You called ordinary, sinful (and perhaps I should add confused) people, but now I'm seeing just how true that is—I get an A in each category.

"God, help me. Prepare Mitch to receive the news. Prepare the people who know us to love us both through this difficult time, and Lord, be our strength in time of need. Give me boldness to be honest. I pray for Mom and Dad, as well, since they have invested money in this wedding and lots of time planning it. Why this? In Jesus's mighty name, Amen."

chapter forty-two

Mitch was apprehensive about this afternoon, but he had high hopes. He knew what was meant by "we need to talk," and he knew from previous conversations with Erica that she knew what it usually meant, as well, making it all the more unnerving. He figured she was going to bring up the topic that he had managed to sidestep for the past month. What she didn't know was that he had been preparing himself for this moment.

Mitch could see Erica's silver car pulling up to his new apartment. He was anxious, his heart beating like a timpani with each step she took toward the apartment. She looked gorgeous as usual, but he could easily read on her face that she came with a heavy purpose.

"Come in, Sweet One. Let me show you what I've done with the place."

He said this in jest. Nothing had been done since he had moved in just three days earlier. Boxes were right where they were initially put, but she did notice that all the dishes were washed and put away from the moving-in supper. That was unexpected.

"I like what you've done with the boxes. Cozy." She didn't seem hostile. That was good.

"I bought something for us." He gallantly led her to the room with the TV, and in there was his new acquisition: a loveseat. The couch was obviously from a garage sale, but the throw covering it was new. She sat down and sank deeply into the cushy couch. Mitch set down two glasses and poured some cranberry juice, topping each with soda water. He served Erica some brie and crackers, and he opened a can of cashews and sat close to her.

Erica apparently didn't know where to begin, so Mitch volunteered to guess what was up and started the ball rolling: "I know we haven't talked like this for a long time, but I've been preparing myself for this discussion. You see, I've been seeing someone—a counselor. I didn't know if it would really help, so I didn't want to say anything earlier. But you know, I feel confident that we can move on in our relationship, and I can give you the affection that you deserve—when the moment is a bit more conducive."

"Mitch, what a brave thing to do. I'm glad you did it." She pushed to make the words sound positive, and then she hesitatingly said, "However, that's not what I came to talk about—at least not just that."

Mitch was hoping for some more interaction about the topic of his seeking counseling, more interest, even thinking exuberance would be nice. He was disappointed but knew he needed to set aside his desires and listen to what she had to say.

"I've been praying about our relationship and believe God has shown me that we need to break our engagement."

There. It was out.

Mitch was not expecting such a straightforward line from Erica, especially not that line. What had happened to the gal he had met over a year ago? He couldn't believe she was being so rude. Where was her much-needed encouragement?

His sarcasm hit the surface: "Why don't you just brand man's six favorite words on my heart."

"What are you talking about? What words?"

"The worst words in the world to hear: I just want to be friends." His face showed pain. Mitch stood up and paced the floor. "Pardon the sarcasm. No, don't. I like the sarcasm. And what's this, now you're using God to break us up? That's not like you. You're better than that."

"Sorry."

"Hey, you're the one who's been showing me how to be more sensitive to people's feelings, and now this, from you? That's a little hypocritical."

Mitch was ready to hurt himself or break something. He was not prepared in the least for this news.

"But it *is* the truth, and I was afraid that if I didn't just say it, I'd chicken out or not be clear enough, and things would just get out of hand."

"Well, I've had my share of talks with God as well, and that's why I got this apartment." He was peering down at her. "Why is He telling me different stuff than He's telling you?"

"Let me back up. Please listen. And have a seat, you're making me feel uncomfortable."

"Fair enough." Mitch sat down, but he distanced himself, practically hugging the armrest.

Erica composed herself. "I asked God for direction about us long before we got engaged. Fast-forward to this past month. Lately, I've been writing down my prayers. As I was doing it this week, the answer stared right back at me. I never wanted to do this, and I guess that's why I didn't do it sooner."

"Do it sooner?" This surely was not feeling fun.

Erica stammered on in a deliberate manner, finally choosing her words carefully: "I am still a bit resentful toward God, actually. He did answer my prayer, but I wish He would have answered it before we got engaged and told the whole world. It would have been so much easier."

"There's something we can agree on. But why do you feel God wants you to break up with me?"

He was calming down from the initial shock.

Erica went into a long explanation, expressing things she hadn't talked to him about since the engagement.

He wanted to say something and cut in: "Can I offer a possible interpretation to your scenario?"

"Sure. Anything."

"I hear what you've been saying, and it even makes sense, I guess. But Erica, you're not being fair. I've been to counseling to work out these things, the very things that have become your big concern. *Now* just doesn't seem like the time to break up, does it?"

"Maybe that would have been true if that had been the only thing, but, as you heard, there's more to it."

He still wasn't convinced. "Erica, maybe God just wanted to see if you'd give me up, like He did with Abraham offering Isaac on the altar. Do you think that could be the case?" He offered the comments with sincerity.

Mitch wondered if she was still thinking about what he said, or waiting for him to say something more.

"No, I don't think that's it." Erica finally had clarity she couldn't deny. In part, she felt like a pawn used by God to bring Mitch to his place of healing. But his words also provided a much-needed understanding of why their relationship had taken place at all. She was finding an element of closure. Now she could see God's hand in having put them together.

Erica had feelings to work out, but she was more convinced than ever that God was making a way for her to go overseas, strengthening her for what would be ahead. She still had strong feelings for Mitch, which made it difficult to say the next words, but she had to.

"I've decided to go to grad school, but first, I need to go back East and live with my parents and save some money. I'm going to call my parents in the next few days and try and set a date to return home—and tell them about us."

Mitch was speechless. He wished things hadn't gone this way. He couldn't picture how he could live without seeing her, nor could he imagine how he'd feel if he did see her at church each week. He desperately wanted to remain friends with her, but he didn't know if that was possible. So many questions were left unanswered for now, but before she left the apartment, she said, "Mitch, I do want to remain friends and hope to keep communication open. And I believe we will, as long as the dialogue remains healthy."

As they hugged good-bye, Mitch leaned down and tenderly, lovingly, gave Erica her first kiss. She slipped away from Mitch's embrace and slowly left, tears streaming down her face. Mitch realized Erica had to keep walking away. He understood that she had left her heart in the doorway of his new apartment. They had both loved each other. That was not in doubt.

Mitch sat, staring at the disconnected TV in his new apartment—the apartment meant for the two of them. He felt the keys in his pocket and stood up, walked outside, got in his car, and headed toward the open road, where he could push the pedal to the metal and clear his head. He blasted some music as he drove, all the while wishing he had some decent speakers. The songs still weren't able to overpower his ability to hear his own thoughts—thoughts that were simply too painful to handle. He headed west on the highway. Once he was outside the city, he began driving way over the speed limit. The sunset that evening was stunning, God's hand-painted masterpiece, but Mitch's vision was too clouded by the pain in his heart to see God's hand in anything at that moment. It was going to take some time.

chapter forty-three

Erica packed her six boxes into her Nissan and drove over to the hotel where her dad had slept the night before. She had said her goodbyes to those at work and from church. She was surprised at how gracious most people had been toward her. Even Johannes spoke kindly toward her, and she was so glad he could be a support to Mitch.

The last few weeks had taught Erica that breakups don't just affect the couple, but their whole sphere of influence—friends, family, places of employment, and sometimes the hopes and dreams of those who observe from afar. The cost of following God's calling affects many relationships. The positive effects were still perhaps years away.

As Erica looked ahead to building her future, she wanted to be sure to keep a link to her past. In Dallas, she had experienced a refining fire—a spiritual boot camp— preparing her for life wherever God would lead her.

Erica's dad turned the ignition key and then put the car in reverse just as "One Pure and Holy Passion" began playing on the radio.

Erica had lots of time to think during the quiet car ride home. However, instead of thinking only about Mitch, the scene that kept replaying in her mind was that of Margie reaching out to hug her as she was leaving. Erica couldn't help but notice Margie's swollen, red eyes. Were they due to Erica leaving or something else?

Although Erica had attempted to build a relationship with Margie, they never really bonded. It wasn't that they had problems or didn't like each other. It was more like their relationship never took off since they were just different from each other—they had different passions, different interests, different lifestyles, different goals, and different philosophies on life. Their relationship was civil, just not close. Erica had decided to accept that, and she felt okay with that, until now. Had she really ever understood Margie? Or had she just assumed too many things? Had she really tried to get to know Margie? Maybe Margie was just shy. Maybe she just didn't know how to tap into Margie's lifeline. She was second-guessing herself. Maybe she had read Margie wrong all along.

The highlight of Erica's last week in Dallas had been meeting Mitch for lunch. While they were eating their salads, he said words she never dreamed she would hear from his lips. Erica had replayed Mitch's comments so many times, they had turned into a personal mantra.

Erica recalled how he had leaned forward, placing the tips of his fingers on hers, and said, "I know you are doing the right thing. Don't harbor any guilt—God will take care of me."

She knew Mitch totally believed what he had said.

These were words of prophecy and promise. Yes, Mitchell Jones was a great man, and he was going to be a great pastor, too.

Again, Erica felt very, very blessed. She was thankful for the chance she'd had to develop a relationship with such a neat man of God. Mitch had only enriched her life, and she had no regrets over her past year with him.

She very much hoped that when he reflected on their relationship, he'd be able to come to a similar conclusion.

Erica's dad drove up to the Super 8, where they would spend the night. Erica's plan had been to go back East, live with her parents, and save money for grad school, hoping she'd find a job quickly. What she hadn't expected was a job offer from her own father. What would it be like to have her dad for a boss and then go back to the same home each night? *God will take care of me.* She clung to that promise, and let her dad know she'd accept his offer. Now she knew they'd have plenty to discuss on the rest of the journey home.

chapter forty-four

Margie reached over to give Erica a hug, wondering who was moving her arms. Sure, she and Erica had spent the past year in the same apartment, but no, this display of affection did not fit her personality, nor their relationship. Margie suddenly experienced a flashback to the evening when she had practically begged Erica to stay on as her apartment mate. It had been an extremely hot night, and all their Bible study guests had just left. Why hadn't she just kept quiet and let Erica go sublet the apartment downstairs? There would have been less emotion to deal with now. Now Erica was not just leaving her, but leaving town, and Margie's teary eyes were betraying her heart. She had genuinely come to care for Erica, hard as she tried to keep their relationship at a distance.

Margie knew onlookers would be curious about her tears. They'd ask each other, "Do you see that? Were Margie and Erica that close? What gives with all the tears?"

Margie didn't understand her own emotions. Thinking back, Erica had been a thorn in her side from the get-go. Why, oh why, did she extend an invitation to her in the first place? She hardly knew her.

Vulnerable was not a word she wanted to be associated

with her; no way. The only thing she dreaded more than feeling vulnerable was having people know how vulnerable she could be. Yes, she should have known better.

Margie could sense Gabriella noticing her tears; tears were natural when change occurred. She watched as Gabriella sauntered over toward her. She felt Gabriella's hand touch her shoulder and heard her whisper, "Can you meet me for coffee at Denny's?"

Margie nodded sheepishly to accept the invitation.

"See you there in a few," responded Gabriella.

Gabriella and Johannes had just given notice to their respective employers. They were going to add yet another change to their status as newlyweds. They didn't have much in savings, but they did have a lot of faith, and they were going to follow the calling they had received. School would start mid-August in Duncanville, Texas. They had already seen their future apartment. It was situated just across from the main center. Their new couch and bedroom set would move with them but remain at the center for others to use someday.

For Gabriella and Johannes, life was pleasantly simple. It was easy to pick up and follow God's leading, no concern about losing many years of investment into a retirement program, no children's school schedule to work around, no house to sell, no pets to find a new home for, and they had each other—no question about who they would end up working with in a translation program. They were free and equipped to follow God.

chapter forty-five

Placing her hands on an antique bench filled with character and charm, Gabriella caught Johannes's eyes and said, "Wouldn't this wooden bench be just perfect for Mitch's entranceway?"

Gabriella was sincere in her finding, but she also knew this would provide the perfect opportunity to check on Mitch. They understood when he hadn't come to say a last goodbye to Erica, but they wanted to check on him nonetheless. They grabbed an energy drink and then headed down to Mitch's place to deliver the bench and see how he was doing.

"Hey, Mitch, you in there?" Gabriella called. "Door's open. We see your car; we know you are somewhere around here."

No answer. Gabriella sat her rear down on the steps while Johannes took a walk around the apartments to see if he could find Mitch.

A few minutes later, Mitch came out from the apartment next door. "Gabriella—!"

She stood up. "Glad you are back. Borrrowing a drill from the neighbor, eh?"

"Yeah. I've got shelves to hang, and I'm replacing a broken shower rod. What brings you here?"

"We have a little something for you." As Gabriella smiled, her eyes twinkled.

"We? Where's Johannes?"

"Oh, he's walking around looking for you, but he knows where to find us. So, more projects! The joys of having your own place."

"I'm not the handiest guy, but I did get that long table to stop teetering. I believe I do more thinking about what needs to be done than actually getting stuff done. I bought a plastic shelf unit for my toiletries. I could use a hand to mark the wall and measure and stuff. Wanna help?"

"Sure. We're always game to practice on someone else's house. Might learn something."

They went into the apartment, and before they even started working, Johannes entered, finding them standing in the kitchenette. Water was the beverage of choice, and Johannes followed suit, pouring himself a glass.

After the shelf unit was secured, Mitch and Johannes went to get the bench out of the car. The phone rang just as the guys put in into place. Mitch grabbed the phone and took it to a quieter place. With Mitch busy with his call, Johannes leaned over to Gabriella.

"So what do you think? Is he going to make it? He needs so much help with this place. Would it be okay if I offer to help him paint the place? That should have been done already."

"Oh, yes. Do it. And how about getting Margie down here? She's got a knack with decorating, and this place could certainly use it. And she's the best when it comes to decorating on a tight budget."

"See if you can sell the idea. I'm not so sure Mitch will go for it."

"Yeah, I see your point." Gabriella turned her head toward Mitch. "Oh, you're back. Who called?"

"The millionth telemarketer."

"Johannes has a great idea—an offer, we hope, you simply can't refuse."

It didn't take but saying the word *paint* to make Mitch's face glow with appreciation. Gabriella immediately sent a text message to Margie to see if she'd be open to helping. After hearing she was, Gabriella invited her down to help them assess Mitch's decorating options.

Margie showed up around an hour later, but by then, no one had energy to think about anything, so they agreed to get together another evening to pick out colors for the rooms and make plans for the window treatments. Pizza was ordered, and they just vegged, chatting away the evening.

chapter forty-six

Mitch made a practice of praying for strength, trying to focus on just the present, and staying very busy. He was getting through the breakup with dignity. He still met with Elmer to work out after Erica left. His hopes of hanging onto a piece of Erica were dashed, and he was also getting an existential shove toward moving on with his life.

Now he spent his days working out at his new complex, studying hard, and reading lots on-line about home maintenance and repairs. Living alone was all so new to him. Last week, his toilet had needed new parts to keep from running. His shopping list also included crystals for a clogged sink and filters for the air-conditioning unit that obviously hadn't been replaced for a while. However, Mitch prided himself the most for his successful installation of a garbage disposal. But when it came to decorating, he knew he needed a woman's touch.

Mitch finally humbled himself to call the all-familiar phone number. As he picked up the phone, his body tensed, and as he pushed the call button, his emotions welled up. He wasn't over Erica—not yet. He knew Margie was the best person for the job, but he still felt a bit awkward about inviting her back to his apartment, even though Gabriella and Johannes would be there too.

Johannes was the first to arrive on Saturday morning. He brought some Krispy Kreme doughnuts along to start the day. Gabriella was feeling nauseous, so she stayed back. Johannes put a fresh coat of paint on the walls, and from the first roller-full, the apartment started to take on a new look. It went quickly between the two of them. Mitch had already put tape around the room, so he was able to start painting around the trim immediately, and they got the first room done in no time. Within a few hours, the whole place had been painted and the doughnuts had been eaten.

Margie had a prior commitment in the morning but had agreed to pick up some sandwiches for the crew for lunch. When she heard Gabriella wouldn't be there, she wanted to renege on her offer, but she knew the guys would need food, so she showed up with a few subs around one o'clock and some fabric and pictures. It was the least she could do after listening to Mitch stammer through asking for her decorating assistance over the phone.

She couldn't help but remember back to the night long ago when Mitch had pushed his way into their apartment. The memory was still so vivid in her mind.

He had been calling Margie for several days in a row, wanting to know how Erica was feeling and asking for detailed accounts of how Erica was acting. His intensity scared Margie a little. He was concerned about Erica, but on this one particular night, he even accused Margie of stirring up trouble for him and Erica, and he demanded to know where she was.

After Margie said she didn't know, Mitch drove over to the apartment, saying he'd stay there till he knew Erica was safe. Mitch was all too aware of how depressed Erica was. She'd been on such a spiritual high just a week before, and now she was struggling with depression again, and they both knew it. She was being distant and noncommunicative—not her usual self.

Margie had played that night over in her mind many times, still remembering it like it was yesterday. She and Mitch were on the couch. Upon hearing the footsteps coming up the stairs, Mitch and Margie panicked, figuring it was Erica. How was she to explain Mitch's presence at the apartment? Mitch wasn't in any shape to deal with Erica at that moment either, as things had gotten out of control.

Erica never did bring up anything to her about having someone over, nor about them hiding under the blanket as they pretended to be asleep. She had simply walked through the room and gone straight to the bathroom, allowing Mitch and Margie to easily escape the apartment and any unwelcome questioning.

Yes, memories. Margie remembered blowing her cool—she downright lost it. She couldn't take another minute of hearing about Erica, Erica, Erica. She finally put her foot down and told Mitch that she'd had enough of his whining and pressure. She didn't want Mitch asking her about Erica or her whereabouts. He seemed surprised, obviously not expecting Margie's sudden angry outburst. Had it been unreasonable and uncalled for, given the stress of living with Erica during that week?

Mitch took the blame. He at least admitted to entering the apartment like a bull in a china shop, insensitive to

Margie's needs. Then he apologized and offered to pray with Margie, and Margie somehow agreed. The time was ripe.

Mitch began by asking God to direct their prayer. Then he asked Margie to feel her anger and asked her if she could identify a time when she first felt that same feeling. She started to sob before he could say another word. Once somewhat composed, she shared about a time when she was with a friend in second grade and the friend wanted her to tell a boy she liked him, but Margie didn't want to. She said it was stupid.

Mitch asked her why she thought it was stupid. She said boys were stupid. It was obvious that Mitch felt uncomfortable about what she was sharing, but he continued to prompt her with questions. At times it felt like probing, but Margie wanted some answers, too.

Around ten minutes later, she remembered a time she was violated as a young girl by her cousin who was babysitting. Mitch touched her hand, and she looked up and saw tears in his eyes. Margie remembered fondly how he was being so very empathetic toward her, so understanding of her need. She felt comforted for the first time.

One vivid scene came to her at the end of their prayer time. She only saw black, but then the black got blacker. It was rich, moving black, like a thick liquid. Then she watched the black go down, down, into the ground. Pouring, pouring. Then she saw a mist, a mist of water, spraying up from the ground. A geyser. And she felt washed over with incredible peace. Lasting peace. *Shalom* peace. God had met her. She sensed the black liquid was the ugliness and sin in her life, and the water was the cleansing of the ugliness. She rejoiced. All this, and then suddenly, the footsteps.

So, the scene was set—just the two of them on the couch, embracing and weeping together. Suddenly, they were hit with the awareness of Erica's untimely return, so they quickly hid under the blanket and feigned sleep. Once given the opportunity, they made their hasty escape to regain their composure and avoid the messy scene of having to explain what was happening.

Since that evening, Margie had felt a certain warmth when she saw Mitch, but she also felt an awkwardness and had avoided eye contact with him. It was the price she paid for being so vulnerable in his presence, but she had been blessed beyond measure that evening and tried to work through the tension. But now that Mitch had called her, she felt it was time to put the past behind her— something she'd always struggled to do. Lunch was about to be served, and there was an apartment that needed some decorating help. This would be her way to pay back to Mitch a little for what he had done for her.

chapter forty-seven

Mitch continued to attend counseling, even after Erica moved away. When he first went to counseling, it was to deal with his inability to be affectionate with her. Then it turned into dealing with his past and the violations that he suffered as a child. Although he had told Erica about them, he realized that back then, he still hadn't been quite ready to face his past the way Margie had begun to face hers. He knew he needed to get to God's truth and healing to get things right, or it would affect his relationship with God and his future happiness as a married man. This had been the focus of his counseling. He needed to get honest with himself, not only about what had happened to him, but about how it was affecting him as an adult. In talking with the counselor, he had initially shared about times of night sweats and panic attacks and even of times he couldn't concentrate on his studies. Now he could look back on the past few months and see how much had changed in his life. He had not only a new home but also a new heart for ministry and a new delight when he opened God's Word.

Margie was able to see all kinds of potential in the apartment and did a great job, in spite of a limited budget. She ended up suggesting a vine-type plant for the living room and some chiffon material to be draped in the second bedroom. She said she had some pieces of wood that would make rustic candleholders for the antique kitchen table.

She had enjoyed her shopping trips, and by now, she was looking forward to when she could admire her vision fully implemented. About five o'clock, they gazed around the room, and it looked like a home. The paint still had to dry, but it didn't seem to interfere with anything other than the hanging of Mitch's two new paintings from Johannes. "Everything looks, great, Margie. You are the coffee to my empty cup."

"Knowing how much you like coffee, I'll take that as a compliment. You were so receptive to my ideas, it made it fun."

"Ha. Compliments that show we complement each other. I couldn't just let that pun go by (or bye-bye)."

"The changes do enhance, I'll agree. Glad we got so much done. See you Sunday?"

"You bet. Thanks, again. Drive safely." And with that, Margie was gone.

chapter forty-eight

Mitch's heart did a flip-flop when he opened his phone. "Erica? Is that really you? How are you? I'm surprised to hear your voice." It had been months since Erica had left.

They exchanged pleasantries, and then Erica's purpose in calling came: "I have some news for you. I didn't expect to return to Dallas so soon, but my parents said they would help me with graduate school expenses. I can start classes in January. I'll only be one semester behind Johannes and Gabriella. I'm planning to update my Facebook status as soon as I get off the phone, and I wanted to be sure you heard it from me before reading about it."

"Okay. Guess that was a good idea."

Mitch had been successful in keeping his heart steady and now wondered if he would be doing as well emotionally once she was back in town. Three steps forward, two steps back. She could really affect his emotional stability. He predicted a sleepless night, wondering about all the possibilities. It was a dead end now that his ex-girlfriend was going to go to the mission field, but he could still hope that just maybe she was looking for a way out and that he might be it. He had to at least entertain the possibility.

Which did he want more: closure or Erica? He wanted God's will in his life and in hers, and he prayed for that to rule.

Erica's time in New Jersey had begun with a conversation between her and her mother in the kitchen, her first morning back. A cherished time indeed—it was the day she felt truly vindicated. Up until then, her plan to go into missions was given nods of approval by friends, but what was her own mother going to think about her baby taking on such a career path? She recounted her journey to her mom, starting with the list she had made about likes and dislikes for a future career, then adding about her experience at church when the missionary came through, her angelic friends Gabriella and Johannes taking her to the school, and even the Mr. Ringing My Chimes lawyer she met on the bus. Her mother was very supportive and even sounded excited for Erica.

Erica's plans were again affirmed in how Pastor Tim immediately started referring to her as "our missionary, Erica." Even her father's circle of work friends praised her altruistic plans. However, her father was not as excited. She didn't understand why, and he didn't offer any reasons. She could only surmise.

It had only been a few weeks, but Erica knew her father enjoyed getting to know her in the workplace. She heard from the secretary that he was really proud of her. A few weeks back, he had told the secretary that he had been apprehensive about hiring his daughter, but he was over that. He found her to be hard-working and a really fun addition to the staff. She was excited to hear this second-hand report, especially after her major flub-ups during the first weeks.

Oh, yes, how was it again? Mr. Webb had gone over to Erica's desk at the new office condo with a request: "Please call and order us some office supplies; we need some more pens and around fifteen reams of computer paper."

"Sure, Dad."

Erica pushed number 3 for fast-dialing and gave in the order: "Yes, a box of black medium point BIC pens and fifteen boxes of legal-size paper. And can you deliver it this afternoon? Great."

The order arrived just after lunchtime. Her father was still out but was expected back soon. When he got back to the office and saw fifteen boxes of paper filling up the only available standing room, Erica heard yelling. "What is all this? Where did this come from? Where am I supposed to store all this paper?"

She hadn't realized there was any problem till that moment. That was the day she learned the difference between ordering a ream of paper and a box of paper. Some very creative organizing took place, and the office was well supplied with paper for the following months.

That wasn't the last of the bad days. Mr. Webb had needed a safety deposit box for the new office mortgage documents and the like, so Erica was given the task of going to the bank to get one set up. The signatures for the box would be her father and Mr. Ricky, his vice president, so she took papers back and forth between the office and the bank, getting needed signatures, finally securing the box. However, when she went to put the important documents into the box, she couldn't find them.

Erica confided in Mr. Ricky, who tried to help her retrace her steps. It seemed the only logical scenario was that the documents just blew out the window of the car while traveling back and forth, or they had gotten left at the house. He sent her home to look, thinking this would be the best scenario. No luck.

Mr. Webb needed to find out, so Erica worked it out with Mr. Ricky to have him tell her father. A week passed, and life was tension-free. She would go home each night and back to work each day, and her father never said a word about the lost documents.

She was so impressed with how her father was handling this awful situation, she took the opportunity to tell the vice president.

"Mr. Ricky, you won't believe how cool my dad has been about the whole documents thing," she said. "He hasn't said a word to me or even made me feel in the least like I disappointed him. Prior to this, I had worried about working for him. No more. He's being so—."

Before she could finish, Mr. Ricky began to laugh hysterically, doubling over.

"What's so funny?" she asked, confused. "Did I say something funny?"

"Oh, Erica. You and your father are a gas to work with," he said. "I had a similar conversation with your father just this morning. He approached me, all bothered because he said you still hadn't admitted you lost the papers. I then clarified that you and I had talked together, and I had agreed to tell him, which is what I did. Then he understood. But apparently this whole week, he was waiting for you to mention it to him. He didn't think you knew he knew. Oh, I am really enjoying this. It's quite the change to have Mr. Webb's daughter working here. I've never seen him act this way. You have quite the effect on his style of leadership, Erica."

"I guess."

She could now look back and laugh over this situation,

since the papers were eventually found; the documents were in the office the whole time. At the end of the month, when Erica went into the file drawer, she noticed some papers had slipped down beneath the files—the very papers she had been looking for everywhere, even there. The safety deposit box was no longer empty.

After Mr. Webb hired Erica, he basically had one rule for her to follow: "No witnessing at work." At first, she couldn't believe her ears; he was going to restrict her from what she thought was the most important duty and delight of a believer?

She remembered the day it got to be an issue. It was a Thursday, two months after she started working for her father. During this particular break time, she got into a discussion that led to her being asked about her spiritual life by Eddie, a new engineer who was just hired. He was young, single, and cute, but she wasn't interested in dating—for once.

She chose to obey her father and simply said, "My dad doesn't want us using company time to discuss personal matters, but if you like, we could get together after hours and talk some more. If it's okay with you, I'd like to postpone our discussion so we can get back to work."

Eddie was fine with this arrangement, and Erica met him at a delightful French restaurant of his choice the next evening. Her father felt the best witness at work was to do the job you were hired to do, no compromise. It was an issue of integrity. One point for Dad's way.

Their date at the restaurant was fun, and they had plenty of time to discuss spiritual issues. "Eddie, you show yourself to be a seeker. Keep pursuing truth."

"How do you suggest I do that?"

Erica saw the waitress and motioned for a refill of her coffee. "John 17:17 in the Bible says, 'Thy Word is truth.' Buy yourself a modern translation of the Bible and read the book of John. Better yet, start with the short book of Galatians. I quoted from that one a lot this evening. It answers several of the questions you asked."

"Modern translation?"

"Try the NLT, which stands for New Living Translation. It's a good place to start your quest for truth."

"I'll think about it."

"May I pray for you?"

"I guess so. Not sure it'll do any good."

"I don't think it'll do any harm." Erica prayed a short prayer.

The check came. Eddie paid, and they called it a night.

chapter forty-nine

"Erica, could you keep your voice down?" came the request from Mr. Ricky.

"What do you mean? Am I—"

"It's just that Eddie has a hangover. He can't handle noise this morning."

"Oh." Erica didn't feel very sympathetic and didn't want to be so nice, but she realized it would be the kindest response.

She remembered how just the day before, she could have used some quiet. Someone had made a poor decision on one of the job sites, and Mr. Ricky was yelling over the phone. It made her feel uncomfortable. Earlier, she had been asked to run an errand to the DMV. At first, she didn't feel like leaving, but the yelling gave her the motivation to get away from the ugly situation in the office. Unfortunately, the stress of the morning, mixed with some cigarette smoke outside the DMV, found her driving back to the office only to pull over and barf on the side of the road. Some days never did get better. She wondered if Eddie would end up barfing.

Other days were joyous, like when the company won the bid on a new contract. The secretary from across the hall came over with champagne to celebrate the victory. A big to-do was being made about the celebration to take place as soon as Dad returned from lunch. Erica's family never drank at home, but this was her father's turf. Was he going to join in the celebration? Would he expect Erica to join in? Or not join in? Even when the glass got to Erica's lips, she still wasn't sure what would please her father. What would be the most respectful action under the circumstances? It just remained ambiguous. Erica took a sip, but left the rest, as did her father. She and her father never discussed it.

So did Erica still want to work for her father? The negatives were minor, and it had turned out to be the thrill of a lifetime. She had grown up always hearing about bids and contracts and estimates and foremen and steelworkers, but she didn't have a clue what her dad actually did that got him so excited about his work. Now she knew. Erica's first bid day was so memorable. Bids were called in, and modifications were made up until the last seconds. The room was suddenly electric with excitement and activity. She would even end up on the phone, asking for the latest numbers from the subcontractors. Everyone was involved.

She didn't want to leave the office life, but she had a calling that was far removed from the construction business. Her father's friends and co-workers showed support of her plans to work overseas, but he hadn't been so supportive. In fact, it was another topic that they never discussed. Finally, Erica had to remind him that she was still planning to leave and asked if he would soon hire someone to replace her.

The conversation hadn't gone as planned. Sure, she understood that her father had spent considerable time in World War II on islands near where she would eventually be going to work. Just two days ago, she spent her evening looking over his scrapbook from the war while he enjoyed a game of cards with friends in the adjacent room. She felt physically ill. It had made her feel sick to read many of the accounts of attacks, conditions, and deaths, and the few pictures made it all so real. But it wasn't only his past war experiences that made him struggle with her calling.

She knew she would always be Daddy's little girl. Oh, had she been a boy and ended up going overseas and dying for a cause, her father would have been heralded as having raised a hero. But she wasn't a boy. She was a girl; it was his responsibility to protect her. There would be no honor if something happened to her, and she and her father both understood that in the silence.

Mr. Webb had heard Erica and responded gently, "Erica, I can't imagine this office without you. You're doing a fine job with the books, and I'm not getting any younger. This company is waiting for you." He choked. "All you have to do is say yes, and it is yours."

She was dumbfounded. How could she? How could he? "Dad, I don't know the first thing about running a construction company. You know that. I'd need an MBA at least and mo—"

"You just need to pray for wisdom and hire the right people. You can do that. You have instinct. Stay on, and you'll learn the business and grow your confidence. You'll see."

Erica was tempted. After all, hadn't she studied business in college? That evening, she tried to picture her future, staying on in New Jersey. She envisioned a life of privilege. She could see herself enjoying vacations yachting on the French Rivera, powerful and rich, but also feeling very alone. She couldn't picture herself the beloved boss. She saw herself isolated in self-protection of her image, her person, and her profession. She saw herself never getting married. She saw herself in a mud hut with a computer.

Before falling asleep, she prayed her father would give her his blessing. She knew it'd break his heart, but the next day, she would officially decline his offer.

chapter fifty

A month before returning to Dallas to continue her schooling, Erica started to train Cyndi, her replacement. After work, they would go play racquetball or attend aerobics classes. Suddenly, it was so tempting to want to stay; for once in her life, she had a companion to keep her active. Cyndi was married, but since her husband was always studying, she had her evenings free. They enjoyed talking about the company and their respective families, and they shared a lot of laughs as well as wisdom. It seemed like a sister had finally entered her life. She had Sherilyn, but Sherilyn was older and lived too far away to just hang after work, plus she had her own family to take care of. Cyndi felt like the missing piece in her life. Now the life she was leaving seemed to hold so much hope, so much temptation to stay.

The day finally arrived for Erica to return to school. She packed up her car and headed to Dallas with Wally. She had heard from Margie that Wally was visiting his family in Camden, and he offered to help her move back down to Dallas. Things were now just fitting into place so well, too well. She knew Somebody was orchestrating it all. Erica and Wally had ended their relationship abruptly just over a year ago, but for a good reason. She didn't know if he was dating anyone now but hoped his current situation wouldn't be a concern. At this point, she wasn't dating anyone, and she didn't think Wally would fit into her plans for missions.

The two-day ride down to Dallas proved to be a wonderful opportunity for Erica to tell Wally about her plans to do Bible translation. He ended up giving Erica his sincere blessing. He sheepishly admitted that when Margie had first told him about her plans to go into missions, he had had a momentary lapse back to being a pompous ass and told her, "Well, I guess Erica's going to serve God since she can't have me." He humbly apologized to Erica for his comment.

Erica got emotional upon seeing the familiar Dallas skyline. They arrived at Wally's place first, and he removed his small suitcase from the back of the car. He leaned over to give her a peck on the cheek. She felt good about how things had gone. She continued on to her school. She arrived before dark, which was her goal. She put a few boxes into her new room and met her new roommate, Brittney. They went to dinner together on the campus and hit it off right away. Erica felt especially blessed as she was mourning the loss of Cyndi. God had been so good to her, and she was flying high once again, experiencing *shalom*.

chapter fifty-one

TWO days later, while driving to the DMV, Erica looked down to check the map and scribbled directions she had been given. As she glanced down, she was quickly reminded to look up. The car was rumbling across a set of railroad tracks. As she looked up into the blinding noonday sun, she could barely see the side of an approaching semi truck; she also saw her life pass before her very eyes. She was heading straight into the side of the truck and quickly slammed on the brakes. She skidded, tensing her body, closing her eyes. She hit, jolted, smashed, turned, and recognized stillness. Her car stopped in the middle of the street.

Suddenly the center of attraction, she realized she was alive. She had experienced a three-point landing on the steering wheel, her forehead making the third point of landing. Everything seemed surreal. A policeman was already at her car, opening the door. People all over were out of their vehicles. Time seemed to stand still. The movie of still pictures flashing before her eyes was gone, replaced by internal questions of what next, what had happened, and what would be the ramifications.

The next few moments seemed to disappear in a haze

of confusion. The next thing Erica knew, she was driving back to her school, perched high above the crowd, sitting in a tow truck, tears finally surfacing. She felt every eye on her as she passed through the gate. What a way to start a semester.

chapter fifty-two

Erica was stiff after the accident and felt very sore for around a week. Her eyes were black and blue, and she had a bruise on her forehead, but there were no broken bones. With the help of her bangs and a few days of healing, she was no longer getting asked, "What happened to you?"

Brittney's little white VW bug was going to be Erica's main mode of travel for the near future. Having to rely on her roommate to get around helped them develop their relationship even more deeply. They were known as best buds within weeks of school starting. Back and forth, doubts and confirmations—her life felt like a wave, tossed to and fro.

With all the excitement of the accident and trying to get her vehicle fixed, she hadn't gone to her old church on the north side of Dallas. Instead, she and Brittney visited lots of different churches. Brittney took her to Church on the Rock, Beverly Hills Church of Christ, Christ for the Nations, and Oak Hill Bible Fellowship. She also attended a rather charismatic Bible study led by one of their professors, Mr. Ellis. One night during the worship, Erica left the group and went outside for some fresh air; she had a little talk with God alone under the breathtaking

Texas sky. Car-less and concerned about her future, she reminded God about all the miracles she'd heard He did for missionaries ever since she was young.

"Lord, will You really be there for me when I go overseas? Will you meet my needs? I'm sure I'll have plenty. And right now, I feel like I need a deposit, an assurance that You will treat me like all the other missionaries I've known. I have an idea for You to consider to help me with my doubts. Will You provide me a car? You know, first my car gets totaled, then I buy it back; I finally get it back all repaired after a very long wait, only to have the block crack since I didn't have enough coolant. At least I still have fifteen hundred dollars from selling it to that mechanic. I hope he can get it fixed for his sake. So, here's the deal. Would You give me a miracle, a deposit so that I can know You will be with me when I leave America and go overseas? I want to ask You for a car—something I would have to consider a miracle if it happened. And one more stipulation: Please don't have my parents involved in helping me with it. I need a miracle that doesn't involve them; I'm sure you understand. With faith, awaiting Your miracle. In Jesus's name, Amen."

The following Friday, while Erica and Brittney were out getting a bite to eat, Brittney told Erica about a Christian used car salesman, and on a whim, they went to his dealership. It was already getting dark when they found a big, old grandma car for $2,000 and were ready to sign papers when it started to rain. A couple was walking around in the lot, and the salesman wanted to talk with them before the rain scared them away. Knowing he had a sure sale with the girls, and fearing the couple would leave, he asked if Erica and Brittney could come back in the morning to complete the transaction.

That evening, Erica was in her room with Brittney when Gabriella called. She walked out into the hallway for some privacy, as it seemed like Gabriella had something serious to say.

Erica heard, "Johannes and I have been praying, and we feel led to give you our old Bobcat. You can do whatever you want with it—sell it for cash, drive it, anything. Just accept it from us as a gift."

Erica's heart was beating fast, her face was flushed, and she had tears in her eyes. With a choked-up voice, she simply thanked Gabriella (and God) for the wonderful gift—her very own miracle. She wasn't ready to explain all it meant to her, not just then. In a semi-daze, she walked back to her room and found Brittney, who had known about her prayer; when she told her what had happened, Brittney said it all in three words: "Isn't God good?"

The next day, Brittney and Erica went to the car dealership to share the bad news and the good news. Since the owner was a believer as well, he was able to rejoice with them, even if he lost the sale. Erica bought a little rainbow appliqué and put it on her car window to remember God's promise to be with her and meet her needs when she was ministering somewhere over the ocean. He was a God to be trusted, a God of miracles.

Erica was not only being exposed to charismatic churches, but she was also reading charismatic books like *From Prison to Prayer* and regularly asking God for clarity on her spiritual gifts. One night, she was driving her Bobcat on the highway and had the idea to speak whatever language came out. It was gibberish to her ear, but then she asked God to give her an interpretation of what she was saying. At that moment, the most beautiful flow of praises to her Father poured out. It was effortless. Had she truly been speaking in tongues? The interpretation of the gibberish never occurred a second time, however. At times, she wondered whether she had a gift of tongues or a personal prayer language. She wasn't really sure what to do with it, either. It was sort of like wanting to get married, begging God for a husband, then one day being married and having no clue what to do, having never thought past the wedding day. Erica asked more questions about tongues and finally decided that if she felt led to practice tongues, she'd do it as an act of faith and obedience. If she didn't feel prompted, she wouldn't.

chapter fifty-three

Now that Erica was back in town and back at church, Margie wanted to know if Mitch had ever told her about the evening they spent together in the apartment. Mitch and Margie had never spoken of that night under the blanket, not until now. He then confided to Margie, "Well, it was the one secret I never felt free to reveal to Erica, but I had always planned to when the time was right."

Margie admitted, "Mitch, it was a very special time." She choked up a bit. "It was as if I felt the Lord feeling my pain, and then it was just gone."

"The Lord does that, Margie. I was just His tool." He and Margie continued to talk, and then he asked her a difficult question: "I've always wondered why you never seemed to get along with Erica. Do you have any idea? I mean, you didn't seem like enemies, but you never got close, either."

Margie knew the real answer and figured it was time for him to know too. "Well," she began, "when I invited various people to move to Dallas, I really didn't think through having someone stay long-term, I guess. I didn't think about the inconvenience. Remember, I'd been living on my own, and I was used to it. My place is only a one-bedroom apartment with one closet—it's really small. It was like suddenly going back to my college days. I felt like I was being sent back to a place I'd already left. I rather liked living alone, and at first, Erica just affirmed that. But toward the end, I guess I started to need her, even though I didn't really know how to depend on her because I was so independent." Working up courage, she asked, "Do you remember what it was like before Erica moved in?"

"What do you mean?"

"Remember the weekend the singles went canoeing. You were a stitch. I had so much fun with everyone. You made me feel alive with every tease, every splash. And you were so strong when I felt too weak to continue on. We not only had fun, we canoed down the river effortlessly with your strength and skill. Well, I sort of found myself attracted to you after that." Margie dropped the first bomb. "So, you see, when the one person I liked, you, got snagged up immediately by my own roommate, Erica, it was quite hard to handle. I was mad at you. I was mad at her. I was mad at myself for inviting her. I was probably mad at God, as well. You had been so friendly toward me that weekend, and many times after that, and then I had to watch you and Erica develop the kind of relationship I wanted with you. I know I wasn't very nice to you during those days."

Margie couldn't believe she had just said it all, nor could she believe how easily it had all flowed out. She had nothing to lose but her pride, and that hadn't been helping her.

"What can I say? I didn't know. Should I apologize?"

"Of course not. Can you believe I even tried to get Erica a new guy so I could have a chance at you? I had it all planned. Remember when she called you about helping a guy learn about dating a Christian?"

"No. When was that?"

"She said she was going to tell you. You mean she—she, well—Wally was a guy I had met through work. It was all Wally's idea, sure, but I was happy to see it happen. I've said enough. You need to talk to Erica if you want details."

Mitch's head was spinning. Erica was in his past and bound to stay there. No need to dredge up stuff now. He pushed down the anger of feeling deceived by Erica, and then he moved on to feeling guilty about misreading Margie all this time. He did remember liking her back then, but he was shy and so was she, and nothing much developed. Of course, Erica entered, catching Mitch's eye the day they were introduced. He pushed that memory from his mind as soon as it came. He was confused for a moment, but at the same time, it all made sense for the very first time—everything that hadn't made sense before.

Mitch suddenly felt like sharing a secret of his own with Margie. Remembering how vulnerable she had been the night he was with her at her apartment, and again now, he finally shared about his own childhood abuse. He ended his story with his belief that he had gone and bought his apartment because he was sure God had told him he was going to be married soon, but sadly, that hadn't happened.

Mitch suddenly had an epiphany; he sensed confirmation about the apartment again and assurance that God had told him he'd be getting married soon. How soon was soon? It was all happening so fast, but suddenly, it made so much sense.

Margie—the woman who understood his weakness, the woman he understood in a special way, the woman he kept finding in his life. They had both been through so much; they had both shared a life with Erica. Now, they just might enjoy spending a lifetime together.

Taking one day at a time, that was how it would go.

Mitch's thoughts bombarded his head as he shared his story, and with tenderness, he continued his story: "My life has just been laid bare before you, Margie. This may seem crazy, but it seems like asking you to marry me is just a formality to what has already happened in my heart. Margie, would you like to pursue …"

He didn't even get his question out before they were enveloped in a kiss. Margie had waited too long for this moment and could not wait any longer. She led the way, and Mitch richly and joyfully reciprocated.

about the author

Janine Hegle spent 20 years abroad between Papua New Guinea, Indonesia, and Peru. She has trained national Bible translators, taught high school English and electives, and been involved in short-term accountant jobs. She continues to be amazed at this thing called grace.

Printed in the United States
By Bookmasters